SAVED

BETH YARNALL

SAVED

ebook ISBN: 9781940811918

print ISBN: 9781940811574

CHAPTER 1

Lucas watched Mi sleep. She looked so fragile and pale against the stark, white hospital sheets. He'd fanned her hair over the pillow, smoothing it away from her face. A bruise was just beginning to bloom on her cheek. He ran a fingertip lightly over it. Her bottom lip was cut. He touched his finger to it as well, willing it to heal, hoping she didn't hurt. He looked down to where her hand rested in his, so small.

He'd been through some shit—some real bad shit—and finding Mi through the chaos and smoke in the studio had been right up there. His chest tightened with the memory of the blast, of not being able to find her. And then when he finally did, she'd been half covered in debris from the set. He'd had a bad moment as he'd dropped down beside her. It was like Gooch all over again. And then she'd opened her eyes and his heart had taken a hard knock against his ribs.

Since then he wouldn't leave her and had made them sew up the gash on his forehead at her bedside. She would be all right. He thanked God or whoever for that miracle. One of the light bars had fallen across her legs. Luckily the couch had taken the brunt of the hit, saving her from any broken bones. She'd hit her head, but escaped with only a slight concussion. There were other injuries, all minor. She'd be bruised and sore, but otherwise okay.

She was damn lucky. They both were. Others hadn't been so fortunate. A cameraman had been burned badly. Another's leg had been crushed. He was still in surgery. Crosby had a broken arm and a severe concussion. Cal had escaped with nothing more than cuts and bruises. His honey hadn't faired so well with cracked ribs and a broken collarbone. Almost no one had escaped unscathed. Considering the size and timing of the blast it was a miracle there wasn't more than the one fatality.

He kissed the back of Mi's hand, marveling at the gift of that simple gesture. Her eyelashes fluttered open. Her gaze searched, then settled on him. His heart felt ten times too big for his chest.

He squeezed her hand to hide the shaking. "Hey."

"Hey." She croaked. "Water?"

He scrambled for the cup the nurse had left. Pressing the straw to her lips, he sent out another silent message of gratitude. She took a few sips, then settled back on the pillow.

"You don't have any broken bones." He tried for cheerful. "Only a slight concussion. They want to keep you overnight for observation."

"I know. I was there when they poked and prodded."

"Right."

"Are you okay?"

"Me?"

Her expression softened at his astonishment. "Yes, you." She eyed the bandage on his forehead. "Is that all?"

He put a self-conscious hand over it. "Yeah. Pretty much."

A frown formed between her brows and she looked as though she was trying to riddle something out. "I'm not sure of what is real. I remember being thrown back, hitting. The heat. Then you were there. Did you take me outside?" He nodded to confirm her memory. She put her free hand up to her ear. "My ears are ringing."

"Mine too. It'll get better."

"Okay." She tried to bite her lip and winced, blinking at the pain. She took a breath. "I think I faded out some. I heard one of the nurses say something about a bomb?"

"Yeah. They think one of the ah, vibrator things had been rigged."

"But why? Why would someone do that to us?"

"People do some fucked up things." He placed her hand between both of his more for his comfort than hers. "For some very fucked up reasons."

"You're quite the philosopher."

"I'm glad you can joke." He grinned at her, feeling for the first time since the explosion that things might turn out all right. "I predict a full recovery."

She gave him a small smile, but the frown still lingered between her brows. "I need you to tell me. I need to know. I saw..." Her eyes filled with tears. "Davy." Her voice broke on a sob. "Is he... did he..." She clamped a hand over her mouth as though keeping the words in kept them from being true.

He rubbed her hand between his, wanting more than anything to not say the words he knew would grieve her. "He didn't make it."

Tears spilled, flowing down her cheeks and around her fingers. Behind her hand she asked, "Who... who else?"

"Just him."

She closed her eyes, her hand forming a fist that she bit. "Crosby?" she managed to squeak out.

"A concussion and broken arm. He'll be okay."

"Tracey?"

"I haven't seen her. She might have been taken to another hospital."

She averted her face, pulled her hand from his and turned away, curling into a ball. "Oh, God, Davy." Her slight frame shook with silent sobs.

He rose from his chair and stood over her, not knowing what to do. Uselessness and despair ate at him until he thought it would consume him. A fine sheen of cold sweat broke out across his forehead. He put a tentative hand out, then pulled it back. He racked his brain for the right words, but none came. Acting on instinct and desperation, he climbed into bed with her. She turned into him. Wrapping his body around her, he brought her in tight.

"I'm sorry, *querida*," he whispered. "I'm so, so sorry."

He'd failed her. He was supposed to protect her. Instead he'd left her exposed, wrongly thinking she'd be safe inside the studio. The cops hadn't said it, but the implication was that the bomb had been meant for Mi. Something about a phone call claiming responsibility and the fact that the product the bomb was in had moments before been on the table in front of Mi. Davy had saved her by switching it at the last moment. He'd lost his life in place of Mi's.

The thought of losing her sunk a hole so deep in him he could hardly breathe. The feel of her safe in his arms, trembling with shock and grief, was a gift he didn't deserve. She gripped the front of his torn and stained shirt, tugging handfuls of his chest hair. He focused on that small pain as a way back to now, back to what he needed to do.

Mi thought she'd dissolve under the weight of her despair. *Davy*. She fisted her hands in Lucas's shirt, trying to find her balance. Davy's face with his shy smile and gentle hazel eyes superimposed over the last image she had of him, lying limp and lifeless just feet away from her. Squeezing her eyes tight, she tried to blot out the memory. She sniffed and swiped at the tears, forcing them back. She never cried, hadn't cried once in the past thirteen years.

Smoothing the wrinkles in Lucas's shirt, she fought for her bearings, fought to make some kind of sense of what had happened. She let out a breath, so thankful for this big man who had come to mean more to her than he should. After the explosion, she'd tried to get to him. He was the first thing she'd thought of. And then suddenly he'd been there, filling her vision. She closed her eyes at the memory that burned so sweet amongst the horror.

She'd turned so easily into him, into the comfort he offered. She sought him out from the moment she opened her eyes in the morning until she closed them at night. She'd come to depend on him. And that scared her down to the deepest, quietest place inside her. She wanted him, could feel herself leaning hard on needing him. He deserved better than she had to offer. Which wasn't much more than her body and the beginnings of feelings she couldn't follow through on.

"I'm sorry about your friend."

He placed a hand on her cheek and swiped a tear with his thumb. She couldn't seem to keep the tears from flowing. He followed it with a kiss to her forehead.

"I just can't believe... he was so young." Her breath shuddered on a suppressed sob. "He would've turned twenty-one next week. Oh, God. His parents. Has anyone called them?"

"I'm sure the cops will take care of that."

She nodded.

He pulled away. "You should rest, *querida*." He climbed out of bed and moved to the window. Hooking a finger in the curtain, he looked out. "The media is camped out in front of the hospital. The explosion will make the news."

"I'm sure Cookie Dixon and the other members of C.A.L.M. will be thrilled." She swiped at another stray tear. "They'll probably get that law reinstated, banning the sale of adult toys in Texas. We'll all be out of jobs." Memories of flames and smoke coming out of the studio filled her mind. Another tear slipped down her cheek. "If we're not already."

"They're claiming responsibility for the explosion."

"God," she said on an exhale.

"The bomb had to have been put in place by someone on the inside."

She whipped her head to look at him, shocked. The pain nearly split her skull. She breathed past the pain. This was all so unbelievable. "One of us did this? Killed Davy?"

He nodded, still looking out the window.

"Who?"

"I wish I knew."

"Do the police?"

"I don't know. What little information I have I got from the detective who came to interview me earlier while you slept."

She lay back in the bed, overwhelmed by this new information. Someone she worked with, someone she saw everyday had tried to kill them. They'd been like a family. Which one of the faces she had thought of as a friend's had harbored a hatred so black they'd kill?

Detective Rolls pushed into the room. He looked like he'd pulled his outfit from the bottom of the hamper and then slept in it. Grimness floated in a cloud around him. The door whooshed closed behind him, bringing the stale scent of dinner trays from the hall into the room. He fixed his bunched up eyes on Mi and sighed. "You look pretty good, considerin'." He motioned toward the chair by the bed. "May I?"

She smoothed away the traces of tears and inclined her head. "Do you know who did this?"

"I wish. ATF recognized the bomb signature, but the guy's been dead more 'an ten years," Rolls said.

Lucas turned away from the window. "Apprentice?"

Rolls jerked in surprise, clamping a hand to his chest. "Jesus H. Christmas. How in the hell d'you do that? I didn't see ya at all. That some special forces shit?"

Lucas scowled in response.

"Apprentice?" Mi asked.

"Most bombers work alone, but if he was with a militant group, he might have had an apprentice, someone to pass his trade on to," Lucas answered.

"That's an angle ATF's trackin'." Rolls took out a notebook and pen. "I haveta ask ya some questions 'bout the bombing."

Mi leaned back against the pillows and pulled the sheet up higher on her chest.

"Are you cold?" Lucas asked her, starting toward the bed.

"No. I'm fine. Thank you. Go ahead with your questions, detective."

Rolls shifted in his seat as though he was settling in for good long while. "Start me off by tellin' me whatya did when ya got to the TV studio."

"From the time we walked in the door?"

"Uh-huh."

Mi smothered a sigh and told the detective everything she could remember. Lucas stayed by the window, alternately looking out and keeping an eye on her. He frowned when Mi described the blast.

"Can ya think of anyone who'd do this or help someone do this?" Rolls asked.

"No." She rubbed her forehead, straining to come up with a clue or something that might help. "I can't believe someone I worked with would do such a thing."

"That's enough," Lucas said, coming away from the window. "She needs to rest. We'll call if we think of anything else."

"Just one more thing," Mi said. "Can you tell me which hospital they took Tracey Casey to? She's the makeup artist for the show. And my friend."

Rolls consulted his notebook. "Casey, you say?"

Mi nodded.

"Don't see the name here. She at the studio when the bomb went off?"

Mi twisted the bed sheet. "Yes."

"She ain't listed as injured." He flipped through the pages some more. "That's odd. She ain't listed as a witness either. You're sure about her bein' there?"

Lucas stepped over. "She was there."

"I'll look into it." Rolls slapped his notebook closed and rested his arms over his belly. "Just so's ya know, we haven't had any luck trackin' down Gann. No credit cards. He hasn't contacted known associates. Nothin'. Just thought ya should know." He stood and awkwardly patted her arm. "Feel better."

Mi stopped him before he left. "Detective?" Rolls turned with his hand on the door handle. "Davy Johnson. Have you notified his family?"

Rolls hangdog face drooped even more. "A few hours ago."

"Could you let me know about his service? I'd like to go."

"Yes, ma'am. I will."

"When you find out about Tracey, you'll let me know that too?"

Rolls nodded. "Ya'll take care." With that he left.

Lucas took up the chair Rolls had vacated. He propped his elbows on his knees, steepled his fingers and gave Mi a thoughtful look. "I don't think that's such a good idea."

She rolled her head on the pillow, unable to do much more. "What?"

"Going to the funeral."

"Why not?"

"It's going to be next to impossible for me to protect you in a crowd. And with all the publicity, there's sure to be a crowd. You're not going."

Sitting up, she braced herself with her elbows. "Yes. I am."

"No. You're not."

"I'm going."

"Mi. *Querida*, please. You can't go."

"Davy was my friend." She couldn't stop the tears that flooded her eyes. Thirteen years was a long time to hold them in. She worried she wouldn't ever be able to damn them up again. "I have to go."

He stood and helped her lay back down. "Rest now, *querida*. You're tired. We'll talk more later."

Settling under the covers, she capitulated only because she *was* tired. He flipped off the overhead light, kissed her lightly on the lips, then resettled into the chair.

Sliding down, he piled his feet on the end of the bed. His head rested on the back of the chair. He regarded her with a closed expression as if he was trying to guard his thoughts from her. Whatever he was thinking, she had a feeling things were going to change. He'd made some kind of decision or come to a conclusion without consulting her. She wanted to ask him, maybe talk him out of it, because she was pretty sure it was going to piss her off.

~

The following day, Mi was released from the hospital. If she thought she'd had it bad before, she knew different now. Things could always get worse. She'd been sent home in hospital scrubs because the paramedics had cut her clothes. Her purse with her wallet and cell phone hadn't been recovered from the rubble yet. She had no job, no income, which hardly mattered when she had no ATM or credit cards. She couldn't go home. Her family had no way to reach her, which worried her to the point of near panic.

But for all of that she was thankful. She'd suffer all of those things and more if only she could have Davy back.

Lucas drove like a man with a mission. He'd been circumspect at best, an impenetrable fortress at worst. Whatever he was plotting made him ornerier than a bee-stung bear. Or it could have been spending the night slouched in a chair that was two sizes too small. Mi would've bet on both.

"Did you get a hold of Cal?" she asked for the fifth

time, expecting the same answer she'd gotten the other four times. She really needed to talk to Cal.

"He's meeting us at our apartment."

"*Our* apartment?"

"What else would you call it?"

"What it is. *Your* apartment."

He didn't answer for a while, glaring out at the road in front of them. "I had some of your things brought over from your house. Clothes... and stuff."

She sat for a moment and just stared at him. So this was what had been rolling around in that hard head of his. "What stuff?"

"Some of your things. To make you feel more comfortable."

"Who brought them over?"

"I had Malcolm take care of it," he said.

"I wish I'd known. I would have asked him to bring my robe and slippers."

"Are you ever going to tell me why you need to talk to Cal so badly?"

"He's my boss. I need to know if I still have a job. If we all still have jobs. And maybe he'd know about Tracey. I'm worried about her."

His brows dipped toward each other. "I'm sure Tracey's home and fine. Cal will bring the show back when the studio's rebuilt. It makes too much money not to."

"What are we all supposed to do for income until then?"

He gave her a quick glance, then turned back to the road.

"I just need to know if I have to apply for unemployment or get a new job," she explained.

"Why not take the time off?"

"And eat what?"

"How will you explain me to your new employer?"

He was right, darn him. Who would hire a woman who had a bodyguard because she was being stalked? Not that she had any useful skills. She'd been darn lucky to get the job at *Pleasure at Home*. There was no way she could get another job with the same pay. How was she going to make her house payment? Pay her mother's expenses? She had no savings, no fall-back option.

"Stop answering my questions with questions," she muttered.

She hunched over in her seat and pushed the heels of her palms to her eyes. She was so screwed. What was she going to do? Maybe Cal could give her a loan until the studio was rebuilt. She'd have to get a second job to pay him back. Or maybe she could do something at his office or at one of his other companies. God. What was she going to do?

"I don't mind feeding you."

She rolled her head his direction. "What?"

"You asked me what you were going to eat. You don't eat much. I'll feed you."

"That's the least of my worries. How am I going to pay my mortgage and... other expenses? I have to get all new credit cards, an ATM card, driver's license, a cell phone. I need money and the ability to access it."

"You don't need money."

"Now that's just a ridiculous statement," she said. "Everybody needs money."

"You can use my cell phone." He pulled his phone out and handed it to her. "Here."

"How's my family going to reach me? How am I going to reach them without access to my contact list in my phone?" She leaned back in her seat and looked out the window. "Never mind. I'll figure it out."

They rode the rest of the way in silence, the tension so tight you could bounce a quarter off it. Mi couldn't wait to talk to Cal. She needed to know where she stood so she could plan. She needed to check in with her mother and Jason. She should call Lucy; she would have heard about the explosion and was probably frantic with worry. Mi wondered if Lucy knew about Davy.

They rode the elevator up to Lucas's apartment as though they were strangers, not touching or talking. The doors opened and Mi took a step back, clamping a hand over her mouth. Her gaze shot to Lucas. He watched her closely—looking for what— gratitude, excitement, approval?

She stepped lightly into the foyer, looked around. "Wha—? Why did you do this?" She walked over to the second-hand couch that was supposed to be sitting in her living room and fingered the quilt draped over it that she'd gotten at a garage sale. She put a hand to her forehead and swept her gaze over nearly every stick of furniture she owned. In Lucas's living room. If she hadn't noticed the differences in their lives before, they were smacking her upside the head now. He'd actually had the couch positioned perfectly to take in the multi-million dollar view of Dallas. It was wrong, all wrong.

She turned to him. "Why?"

He hitched a shoulder, tucking his hands in his pockets. "I hated that other furniture."

"Where did it go?" She had an image of his expensive, modern furniture in her cracker box tract home and laughed out loud. Then she spotted the grouping of photos on the built-in bookcase and bent over at the waist, gripping her knees. He'd brought them here. *Oh my God.* How was she going to explain them?

"Your furniture is more comfortable. I wanted you to be comfortable."

Her two worlds were crashing together and there wasn't anything she could do to slow it or stop it. Tiny dots filled her vision and a sick feeling sat heavily in her stomach. She staggered, putting a hand out, and came up against the back of the couch.

He rushed to her side. "Are you all right?"

"No. It's too much. You did too much. I can't... Why didn't you tell me?"

"I did. Come and lie down." He helped her to the sofa.

"You said *some things*. As far as I can tell this is everything." She tried not to bring his attention to the photos by looking at them. Instead she focused on the other issue. Was this his way of asking her to move in with him? They hadn't discussed a future or anything beyond now. "How am I supposed to take this? What does this mean?" She held her breath, hoping and at the same time terrified. She wanted this. She wanted him. But as keen as the wanting was, the secret that she kept from him, from everyone, knocked him out of her reach.

~

"You can't stay in your home, but at least you can have your things from there here," Lucas said. "So much has been taken from you, *querida*. I thought maybe having your stuff around might help. Especially after yesterday." Although now in the face of her displeasure, Lucas doubted the wisdom of his actions.

"Doyle Gann could be captured tomorrow and then what?"

"You want it to go back, it goes back. Today, tomorrow, whenever." Not that he wanted it to. For the first time there was furniture in the apartment that he could take a nap on without worrying about bodily harm.

"Seems like a lot of trouble," she grumbled, settling into a corner of the couch. And right there—the look on her face, the way she relaxed, tucking her feet under her, laying her head on the pillow—that's why he'd done it.

He pulled the blanket off the couch and laid it over her, then sat on the edge and looked down at her. She was so pretty, so delicate even with her face dotted with scratches and the nasty bruise on her cheek. He smoothed the hair back from her face. Her amazing whiskey colored eyes fluttered open, zeroed in on his and he felt her as though she were inside him, a part of him. When she looked at him like that he felt powerful and weak, afraid and fearless.

He wanted her so bad, in every way. Couldn't

remember ever wanting anyone or anything this much. Imagining she might want him, he got a little light-headed. Having her here, her things mixed with his, felt right. He wasn't going to look too hard at what he got out of bringing her things here. If he did, he just might have to admit he didn't ever want her to leave or that he had something with Mi that he'd never had with Vanessa.

He was so fucked.

"I'll wake you when Cal gets here." He leaned down and kissed her, resisting the urge to lie down beside her. He wasn't sure he could keep his hands to himself and the last thing she needed was him trying to cop a feel.

She sighed and sank deeper into the cushions, closing her eyes. He sat with her a moment, finding it difficult to leave her. He hadn't felt that with Vanessa or anyone else for that matter. When her breathing lengthened and evened, he forced himself to rise, giving her one last look before heading into his office to make a few phone calls.

Yup. He was well and truly fucked.

CHAPTER 2

Mi woke to the rumble of male voices and the ringing of her cell phone. Her cell phone? There it was, unharmed on the coffee table that had been in her house only yesterday. Sitting, she picked it up. Her phone, but not her phone. A new one. The number on the screen was Jason's. She flipped it open, dread dropping like a rock into her stomach.

"Hello?"

"What the fuck, Mi? Where are you? Are you all right?"

She pounded her knee with her fist. Damn! She should have tried somehow to call Jason after the explosion. "I'm okay. I wasn't hurt."

"The hospital called me. I've been calling and calling you."

"My cell was in my purse at the studio. I had to get a new one." Or rather Lucas had gotten it for her. One more way he'd taken care of her.

"They wouldn't give me any information over the

phone. So I turned on the TV and saw... fuck *me*." She could hear the fear and worry in his voice.

"I know. I'm so sorry. I should have called you. How's Mom?" She suddenly noticed the voices she'd heard when she first woke up had quieted. Turning, she looked over the back of the couch to find Lucas and Cal watching her.

"She's giving *Ethan* a bath."

She got up and went to the window, putting her back to Cal and Lucas. "You're there with her?"

"Yeah, that's why I couldn't go down to the hospital. One of her neighbors called me yesterday. She was doing it again."

"How bad?"

"She needs help, Mi."

"She'll get better. She always does."

"How?" He didn't hold back his exasperation and frustration. He never did. "Face it. She's not getting better. She never does. Not for long anyway."

She rested her forehead on the cool glass. The reflection off a nearby building forced her to close her eyes. "She will. I'll come as soon as I can. Please just stay with her until I can get there."

"I'll spend the night, but I have to go to work tomorrow. She'll be alone after that. I can't leave work to come here every day."

"I know."

"I'm glad you're okay."

"Thanks."

"Yeah."

"And Jason, thanks for the help. I really appreciate it."

"Yeah, all right. I'm still going to kick your ass for not calling me."

She laughed, feeling better. "Like you could. Bye. And thanks again."

"Sure." He disconnected.

She flipped the phone closed. Jason was right. Their mother wasn't going to get better. She'd be all right for a while and then slip back into the madness. It wasn't her fault, Mi knew, but that didn't keep the resentment and anger away. They were as much a part of their relationship as love and acceptance, most days more. Her mother had never been much, but she was all Mi and Jason had.

She turned from the window. Lucas and Cal had gone into the kitchen. She could hear their voices. She slipped the phone in her pocket and followed them.

Lucas leaned against the counter, arms crossed over his chest. Cal had hitched himself up onto a bar stool, sipping a soda straight from the can. His Stetson sat on the counter at his elbow.

Mi slid onto the stool next to Cal. She motioned to Cal's soda. "Can I have one of those, too, please?"

Lucas reached into the refrigerator, pulled a can out and popped the top. He sat it in front of her. "How's your mom feeling?"

She worked to keep the surprise from her face. "She's okay." She sipped the soda, the bubbles bursting on her tongue. "I guess the phone fairy came while I was sleeping."

"Is it all right? I got you the same one you had."

"Yes. Thank you. You didn't have to do that, you know."

"I know." He eased away from the counter. "I'll let the two of you talk."

Cal watched Lucas go, then turned to her. "Do you know why I asked him to be your bodyguard?" He watched her with cool blue eyes that missed nothing. For all his good ol' boy charm, Cal was as shrewd as they came.

"I heard he owed you a favor."

He bobbed his head companionably. "He thought so, but no."

He drank his soda. Mi did the same, waiting him out. With Cal you only got what he felt like giving, when he felt like giving it. She could tell he was working up to something. You didn't rush Cal any more than you rushed a stubborn bull or sunrise. What he did, he did with deliberation and purpose. He hadn't built his empire from nothing by hurrying about chasing ideas or picking up after others, but with calculated intent delivered with the precision of a gem cutter.

"What do you think of what Lucas's done, moving your furniture here?" he finally asked.

She traced a finger over the chipped paint of her Porky Pig cookie jar on the counter next to her, a smile tugging one corner of her lips. "It's strange and over the top, but totally Lucas."

He nodded in agreement, eyeing the cookie jar with some amusement. "It is."

"He does things like that and I think I should be mad. But I'm not. I'm too glad about it to be mad. It's sweet. He's sweet."

"He inherited a lot of money some years back."

Ah, now they were getting around to it. She made a show of looking about as though she were taking a mental inventory, calculating Lucas's worth. "Apparently so."

"Money affects everyone differently."

"'Nowadays people know the price of everything and the value of nothing.'" She quoted Oscar Wilde.

"I see appreciation isn't lost on you."

"Appreciation is the only thing I have to give him."

He examined her as though she was up for auction and he was deciding his maximum bid. "Not the only thing." He tipped his soda to his lips and finished it down. "Loyalty is undervalued."

"Sad, but true."

"To answer my earlier question: I knew he'd guard you like his own maiden aunt. And not just because I asked him to. I knew he'd take one look at you and not be able to help himself. I'm wondering if that was a mistake on my part."

She matched his shrewd look and demeanor as best she could. "Seems like I'm not the only one who needs protecting."

"What did you want to talk with me about?"

And that subject was now closed. "I was wondering what your plans are for the show."

"We'll run old shows, maybe cut and paste some. I'm already looking for a new space, but that will take some time to get up and running."

"What will we do until then?" she asked. "I'm sure I'm not the only one on the staff who has a mortgage to pay."

"My company has insurance for something like this.

I've already contacted my carrier. Workman's comp will take care of the medical expenses."

"Okay." She breathed out a sigh of relief. "You don't know how much I needed to hear that. Thank you."

He slid off the stool and picked up his hat, taking her measure with a slow head to toe scan. "A loan wouldn't be out of the question under the circumstances."

"Unfortunately, I might have to take you up on that."

"Just let me know." He turned to go, then angled back around, fixing her with a beady stare. "I'm hardly ever wrong. Don't make this one of those times."

She lifted her chin, meeting his challenge. "Your record will stand."

He gave a curt nod and donned his hat with a slow practiced motion. She watched him go with new respect. He might have a reputation as a hardnosed businessman, but underneath he was the kind of friend everyone should have.

Sensing she should hang back until Cal left, she remained at the counter, finishing her soda. She pulled the new cell phone from her pocket and clicked 'Contacts'. They were all there. She let out a relieved breath and called Tracey. Her call went straight through to voice mail.

"Tracey, it's Mi. Are you okay? Please call me. I'm worried about you." She hit End more worried than ever. Next she called Lucy.

Lucy answered after the first ring. "Mi! There you are. I've been worried sick. I couldn't get ahold of *anybody*. What happened? They said there was one casualty. How are you? Are you hurt? *What happened*?"

"I'm fine, really. Oh, Lucy. It was Davy—"

"Oh, no."

"He was right near the bomb." Mi's voice broke. She took a deep breath, trying to be strong for her friend. "I still can't believe it."

"Who would do something like this? Who has that much hate in them?"

"I wish I knew. The police think someone at the studio has been sabotaging the show and that same person set the bomb. Someone we know and see every day. I just can't think who would do that."

"I can't just believe one of us could do that. Everyone there is like family. I miss that."

Lucy was going through the same thing Mi had, turning it around, trying to make sense out of something so senseless. There were no answers, only more questions.

Mi talked to her friend for a few more minutes, trying to calm her down. They disconnected with promises to get together soon. Mi clicked the phone closed and swiped at her tears before they could fall.

"Everything all right?" Lucas asked.

"Yes. No. It's just so awful." She indicated her phone. "That was Lucy. I told her about Davy."

He came to her, wrapping her in his arms. "I'm sorry."

She melted into his warmth, his comfort. How had she come to depend on him so quickly when she'd gone so long with no one to rely on? And what was she going to do when the day came when she'd have to do without him?

He smoothed a hand over her hair and she pulled

back a little to look up at him. Yes, indeed, what would she do if he never looked at her like that again? If she couldn't feel his arms around her, his heart beat against hers, his breath over her skin?

She took his hand, kissed the inside of his wrist, then the palm. Such big, gentle hands could bring comfort and pleasure. He watched her, his dark eyes heating, shining with the same desire that flared within her. She flicked her tongue out, tracing a circle over his palm. He moved closer and she widened her legs, inviting him in.

Their lips met in the briefest of kisses, then again before they settled into each other, tongues mating. She reached for him, bringing him closer still and slid her hands into his hair. God, she loved the feel of his hair and the way his body fit against hers. The feel of his hand on her bare midriff added fuel to the fire. She wanted his hands on her, everywhere. Pulling at his shirt, she broke the kiss to trail her mouth down his neck.

"Are you sure you're up for this?" he asked.

"I need this," she whispered in his ear. "I need you."

He shivered, a rippling of muscle. "You got me."

He scooped her up in one motion and carried her back through the living room and down the hall to the bedroom. He laid her down and went into the arms she stretched out to him. She wanted his weight on her, holding her down so she wouldn't fly apart. Needing the feel of skin on skin, she yanked at her clothing, then his. In seconds she got what she wanted, and that first moment when their flesh met settled something inside her, at the same time releasing a current of longing that sent her straight to him.

No one was like him. His hands, his mouth, his body did things for her that no one had ever done, would ever do. After the first flurry of movement to get naked, they slowed things down. His fingertips feathered over her skin, setting small fires in their wake. He savored her, she felt it in the way he looked at her and touched her. This would be no frenzied coupling. It would be slow and deliberate and before they were through they'd each have taken more and given more than they should have. She knew this and yet couldn't stop it, couldn't keep herself apart from him anymore.

She melted into the sensations, gave over to the sweet ride and in return elicited long drawn out sighs and sharp intakes of breath from him that only encouraged more. She pleasured him with her mouth and her hands, telling him with her body what words could never express. Holding nothing back, they gave until they shook with a need that might never be quenched.

And the moment he entered her she knew they'd crossed a threshold, could see it reflected back at her. He whispered words of endearment as he rocked into her, keeping pace with the hammering of her heart. Limbs entwined, bodies slick with sweat, hearts beating out a pounding rhythm they found their release, a shattering climax that brought tears to her eyes. He shook with the after effects and she wrapped her limbs around him, anchoring him to her.

Their breathing slowed, but their hands kept moving, caressing, soothing. They'd been through a war, a rebirth. What they'd be on the other side, she didn't know. She should be scared, but all she could do was accept.

He tucked her tight against him as they drifted toward slumber. "*Mi amor*," he murmured in a voice almost too quiet to be heard. But she'd heard and understood. *My love*.

MI WOKE FIRST, having slept earlier. She shifted in Lucas's arms, wanting to watch him unguarded, still sleeping. The fine lines around his eyes smoothed in relaxation his lips seemed fuller almost pouty. She resisted the urge to touch them, knowing they were softer than they looked. This was the first time she'd really studied him without him knowing. Her gaze traced every contour, every sharp angle. She supposed he wasn't classically handsome, but there was something about him, something basic and masculine that called to everything that was feminine within her.

"It's not polite to stare," he said, his eyes opening and meeting hers in that very direct way he had.

"You big faker. How long have you been awake?"

"Not long."

"You should have woken me up sooner." She smoothed a hand down his body and found him hard. "We could already be working on a way to fix this problem you seem to have." She stroked him, eliciting a moan. "I know just what to do."

Wanting to do something for him after all of the things he'd done for her, she threw off the covers. She kissed her way down up his body, paying special attention to her favorite parts until she arrived at her very favorite part of him. Taking him in her mouth, she coaxed and teased until she knew he was right on the edge.

He reached a hand down to her. "Come here."

"No. Lie back and enjoy. Let me do this for you."

He groaned and said something incoherent as she went down on him again. He watched her with eyes hot and heavy. She took her time, then quickened the pace when she knew he needed it. He came with a jerk and a moan ripped from his throat. Dotting kisses back up his body, she hoped he knew she'd never betray him, tried to tell him without words that he could trust her even when she couldn't be honest.

"Hmm, problem solved," she whispered and kissed him just below his ear.

He rolled them so he was on top, hovering over her, never crushing her. "We've only got twenty minutes, but I'm up for the challenge." Palming her breast, he kissed her neck in that way that drove her crazy.

"What do you mean twenty minutes?" she gasped.

He nibbled her earlobe. "Hmm, before we have to go see my mother."

She bolted upright, shoving him off her. "Your *what*?"

He rolled easily to the side. "I have to make an appearance and you'll have to go with me obviously." He went for her breast again.

"In twenty minutes? Oh, no." She knocked his hand aside and climbed out of bed. "Your mother?" Throwing up her hands she stomped into the closet. "What am I going to wear?"

LUCAS WATCHED HER GO, chuckling to himself at her reaction. He hated leaving the bed, hated more the reason he wouldn't get to return Mi's favor.

She bounced back into the room, gloriously naked and madder than a coiled snake. "Why didn't you tell me sooner?" she demanded. "How long are we staying?"

"We're going for dinner. Come here."

"Dinner! Oh my God. You should have told me sooner."

He craned his neck to take in her backside as she disappeared back into the closet. Yeah, he really hated that his mother had called and insisted he show up tonight. She'd laid the guilt on thick, using his sister's upcoming trip as an excuse to get him there. Not that he didn't want to see his family. He sat up on the edge of the bed and scrubbed his hands over his face. He'd have to explain Mi and he wasn't entirely sure how she'd want to be described.

He leaned forward to see into the closet. She was still naked, frowning over a couple of dresses. He hated them both, knowing one of them would soon be covering entirely too much of her.

She turned to look at him, a frown still creasing her brow. "Which one?" She held up one, then the other in front of her body.

"Neither. Come back to bed, I'm not done with you yet."

"No way." She bit her lip. "I wish I had time for a

shower. I smell like sex." She crinkled her nose like that was a bad thing.

"We can take one together."

"Lucas, be serious."

"I am serious." He got up, went into the bathroom and turned the shower on.

Mi followed him in and gasped when she got a look at herself in the mirror. "My face."

"Is bruised, but beautiful. Come take a shower with me."

"I'm meeting your mother for the first time. I'm not going to show up late because you wanted water play."

"And my sisters."

She whipped her head around and glared at him. "Your sisters? How many?"

"Three."

She slumped against the counter. "Three?"

He nodded.

"Any brothers or other relatives I should know about?"

"I have some aunts and uncles, but they won't be there."

"Thank God."

"Just *Abuelita*."

She gave him a funny look.

"My grandma."

"I'm meeting your mother *and* grandmother? Tonight? With twenty minutes notice, looking like I got beat up, reeking of sex?"

He wasn't sure he should respond, recognizing a potential disaster when he saw one. Instead he opened the shower door and made a motion for her to step in. Her nervousness was cute. He had no doubt that she'd make a better impression on his family than he had with her brother. A situation he'd have to try to rectify the next time he saw the punk.

Half an hour later, they hustled down to Lucas's truck. Mi's hair was still damp, but she'd done something to her eyes that made them sparkle like new pennies. She'd put on lipstick that drew his attention to her generous lips. God, he loved her mouth. And the things she did to him with it. Thinking about those things made his dick twitch so he tried not to think as he helped her into the truck.

He'd filled her in on his family while they got ready. He was the youngest of four and the only son. His parents had divorced when he was young and his father lived in California with his new wife. His mother never remarried. Two of his sisters would be there tonight. His oldest sister lived in Houston with her husband and two daughters. Of his other two sisters, one was divorced, the other unmarried.

"So your ablu— "

"Ah-bwe-lee-ta," he pronounced. "But you'll call her Mrs. Vega."

"So she's your father's mother."

"No. She's my mother's mother. We were given my mother's last name instead of my father's."

"That's unusual."

He kept his eyes on the road. "Yes."

"Can I ask why?"

"There was no choice. *Abuelo* insisted on it."

"Your mother's father?" she asked.

He gave a curt nod.

"Your father didn't have a problem with that?"

"He did. Still does. But my grandfather was a man who always got his way. Always. Eventually my father left my mother, left us, because he couldn't bend to his father-in-law's will any longer."

"I'm sorry."

He shrugged, flicking off the shreds of anger he still carried. "I was named after *Abuelo*. Joaquin Lucas Romero Vega. Romero was my father's addition, his dig at my grandfather, giving his only son his last name. Later after my parents split, *Abuelo* had Romero removed from my birth certificate."

Mi couldn't contain her shock. "That's... selfish."

"That was *Abuelo*."

"When did he pass away?"

They pulled up to a huge ornate wrought iron gate. Lucas turned to her, searching her face in the darkened cab. He ignored the voice from the speaker box requesting their names.

"Three years ago. And before you offer your condolences, you should know that the day they put *Abuelo* in the ground was one of the happiest days of my life. I would have shoveled the dirt over him myself if they'd have let me."

His vehement words delivered with a bald hatred she never knew existed within him, scattered goose bumps over her flesh. She looked at him as if seeing him for the first time. And maybe she was.

CHAPTER 3

Lucas lowered the truck window and gave his name to the guy on the other side of the speaker box. The gates slid slowly open. He rolled his shoulders as though shaking off a weight and stared straight ahead. Mi sat in the cab next to him and wondered what she was in for. Every family had their share of problems and skeletons in the closet—she knew this all too well. But the way he'd talked about his grandfather was almost like a warning as though the man was still alive. She bit her lip, wondering if maybe this was a mistake. And then she got a look at the house and *knew* it was.

Two and three stories high, the mansion rose up from the bricked drive like a great stone Phoenix with its wings spread wide. More than a dozen large arched windows glowed from within as if they owned the power company and could afford to light every room at once. Lucas circled around a tremendous stone fountain set in the middle of the drive like a jewel in a crown and stopped the truck.

Mi looked down at her blouse, peasant skirt, and sandals—perfect for a summer night out with friends—and wished she'd worn her one and only cocktail dress. Lucas's clothes were casual too, but of a much finer cut and quality.

"You look great," he said, breaking into her thoughts.

"They do know I'm coming to dinner with you, right?" She looked up at the front door, massive and intimidating at the top of the stone steps. She was so far out of her element she wasn't even sure she was still in Texas.

He took her hand and kissed the back of it. "They know I'm bringing a guest."

"A guest," she repeated, frowning over the formality.

"How *should* I introduce you?"

She looked at him then, unsure of her response. What was she to him? A friend? Sure. A lover? Most definitely. They lived together out of necessity, not choice. They'd agreed to be exclusive, but they'd never been out on a date. What *did* that make them?

"Guest is fine," she replied.

He climbed out of the truck, came around to her side and opened her door. He held out his hand to help her down. They climbed the steps side by side. Lucas pressed the doorbell.

"Guest is stupid," he muttered.

"Lover? Bedmate? Fuck buddy? Friends with benefits?"

He snorted and slung his arm around her. "Fuck buddy. I like that one."

A woman who looked to be about Mi's age opened the thick door. "Welcome, Mr. Vega." She stepped aside, motioning for them to enter.

Mi tried not to gawk at all the splendor as they followed the woman through the foyer and deeper into the house. Dark wood, crystal, gilt, ornate, Italianate and all other kinds of –ate she could never afford glittered and gleamed. She kept her hands at her sides, holding her skirt, careful not to brush too close to anything.

"Mrs. Vega is expecting you and your guest in The Rose Room," the woman said over her shoulder.

"Thank you, Carla," Lucas said.

The Rose Room, Mi mouthed to herself, trying not to roll her eyes.

They stopped at a set of paneled double doors, which Carla slid open for them. Carla stood off to the side to allow them to enter the room. "May I bring you and your guest a beverage?" Carla asked.

Lucas looked to her. "Mi?"

Mi always thought it best to face the worst sober. "Water please."

Carla looked at her expectantly. "Still or sparkling?"

"Sparkling, please."

"Of course. Mr. Vega?"

"I'll have the same. Thank you."

Carla bowed to them, then went off to get their drinks.

Lucas placed his hand low on Mi's back and ushered her into the room. The first thing Mi thought was, *Why is this room not pink or covered in roses?* The second thing was that she was woefully underdressed *and* under-accessorized. But it was what it was so she plastered on her *Pleasure at Home* smile and ratcheted up her determination that this would *not* be a disaster of epic proportions.

"Lucas!" A woman with long, sleek, dark hair and eyes like Lucas's rushed over to him and gave him a hug. She pulled back and examined his face. "What happened to your forehead?"

"Accident," he replied.

The three other women in the room turned as if one, then made their way over to them. An older woman about the same height as Mi, who could only be Lucas's grandmother, patted and kissed him, murmuring in Spanish all the while. If it weren't for the tightness around his mouth, Mi would have thought he enjoyed her attention. Next came a woman who could only be his mother with threads of gray through her blue-black hair. Reserved in her greeting, she had tears in her eyes as she embraced him. The women continued to fuss over Lucas and his injury as though he was the king of the castle come home. Mi found herself wedged into a corner by their exuberance to be near him.

"There's someone I'd like you all to meet," Lucas finally said, breaking through the chatter. He held out a hand to Mi, drawing her into their circle. He put his arm around her shoulders, bringing her up against him. "This is Miyuki Price-Jones... my girlfriend."

Mi suppressed the twitch of her lips that wanted to be a smile. For a heady moment there she thought he was going to introduce her as his fuck buddy.

"Mi, this is my sister Elisa and my other sister Carmen," he said gesturing to the woman who had greeted him first and then to the other woman who was the tallest of the four Vega women. He continued the introductions. "My mother Isadora Vega and my grand-mother Ofelia Vega."

"Pleased to meet you," Mi said, shaking each woman's hand in turn.

Lucas's grandmother said something to his mother in Spanish, and his mother replied likewise. Elisa rolled her eyes, while Carmen nodded along with what was being said. Mi didn't have to understand the words to know they were talking about her and not in a flattering way.

Lucas's face flushed, his body tensing against hers. "English, please," he said pointedly to his mother. "I know how tiresome you find rudeness."

Carla came into the room, carrying a tray with two glasses and served them to Lucas and Mi. After Carla left, Lucas's mother dropped dramatically onto a nearby sofa with an exaggerated sigh.

His grandmother gave her daughter a disapproving look, then turned to Mi, examining her head to toe. "You are not Latina." Her tone did more than suggest that this was not a good thing.

Mi would have answered, but Lucas beat her to it "No, *Abuelita*. She's not." He sounded weary as if this was a long-standing argument in which there would never be a resolution.

"Mario Ortiz's daughter is in town. You remember her, pretty girl, nice broad hips for lots of babies. She asked about you. I'll phone her and have her join us for coffee and dessert."

"Do that and we won't stay past the first course," Lucas replied with a challenge in his voice that matched the look on his face.

His grandmother reached up and patted him on the chest, which was as far up as she could. Pride showed on her face, softening her words. "So much machismo just like your *abuelo*. God rest his soul." She crossed herself in the Catholic tradition, kissing the locket around her neck as a finale.

"What do you do for a living... Mi, is it?" Elisa asked. Lucas looked at her with a mixture of relief and gratitude for the subject change.

"Yes, I prefer Mi." And here's where it got tricky, Mi thought. People were either repulsed or fascinated by her job. "I'm the host of a shopping show on TSN."

"Oh, I love the Television Shopping Network!" And then recognition dawned on Elisa's face. She gave Lucas a knowing smile and wink, which was quickly replaced by a look of distress. "Oh lord, that's the show that got blown up."

Carmen, silent until now, spoke with a soft voice contradictory to her extraordinary height. "It was on the news and the paper this morning." She looked to her mother. "You remember." Her lips twisted into a smirk. "The show that sells sex toys?"

"Carmen," their grandmother scolded. "Watch your language in my house." Then she turned her dark, wrinkly eyes on Mi, slicing her to ribbons with her laser stare. "Lucas, explain."

Lucas went into a brief explanation of what had been happening at the studio, leaving out the part about his being Mi's bodyguard. Mi tried not to stare at the carpet; keeping her gaze on Lucas with four sets of Vega eyes fixed on her was not an easy task. The air in the room seemed to thicken with condemnation. Mi tried not to twitch under the pressure, listening to Lucas as though her existence depended on it. And it probably did.

When Lucas finished, his grandmother burst into a flurry of Spanish aimed at him. Mi bit her lip; it seemed disapproval was a universal language.

Elisa used the distraction to sidle up to Mi. Putting a hand on Mi's arm, she leaned in to whisper in her ear. "So, do you get a discount?"

"Mostly I get them for free," Mi whispered back.

"I think you and I are going to be great friends." She linked her arm through Mi's and steered her out of the room. As soon as the door closed behind them, Elisa let out a deep breath. "Once she gets going, it never stops. You're lucky not to know any Spanish. Come outside with me." She went on ahead, leaving Mi to catch up.

Mi followed Elisa out to a covered patio, where Elisa leaned against a railing. She pulled a packet of cigarettes out of her pocket and offered one to Mi.

"No, thanks," Mi said.

Elisa lit one up and inhaled, then blew a stream of smoke over her shoulder. She crossed an arm over her middle and propped her elbow on it, holding her cigarette up. "I love your show. You're so good, you make me want to buy everything. Except those things guys use to get off, of course."

She took another puff off her cigarette. "So how did you two really meet? Because I know Lucas, and he's more straight-laced than *Abuelita*. I can't believe he'd go after someone like you. No offense, I think you're fantastic, but it's a wonder he can walk with that stick up his ass."

Mi laughed and it felt good. She liked Elisa a lot, but didn't quite feel comfortable enough to fill in the gaps Lucas had intentionally left blank. "We met on the set of the show, as Lucas said."

"Well then how... oh, right. Cal. Mmm, that is one sexy cowboy." Elisa's opinion didn't seem to need Mi's agreement, because she plowed on ahead with the conversation without her. "She could be at it for hours in there. Much is expected of Lucas, as I'm sure he's already told you. Being the heir and all. And at the top of the list is his marrying a woman of Mexican descent to continue the Vega line."

Actually, Mi hadn't known. Lucas hadn't mentioned anything about his family's expectations. Mi certainly didn't fit in with what his family wanted for him, not that she considered herself in the running. She wondered if Vanessa had met his family's criteria for a potential wife. Mi would've bet money that she had or else why would Lucas have gone out with somebody like Vanessa?

Elisa took a hit off her cigarette, trailing the smoke out slowly, then gestured toward the house. "Ignore Carmen, she wishes she was born a boy so she could've inherited in his place instead of being Lucas's stand-in. But then she would've had to spend hours in *Abuelo's* study learning how to run the family business and wouldn't have had time to read." She put a hand over mouth and stage whispered, "Romance novels." She laughed. "Carmen tries to hide them, but I know and now you know—" She gave Mi a conspirator wink. "—that she likes bodice rippers, the steamier the better." She flicked her cigarette over the railing. "But then, so do I. I sneak them from her when she's not looking."

Mi smiled. "I like them, too."

Elisa smiled back. "I just knew when I saw you, we were destined to be friends. You're much better than that bitch Vanessa. Prettier, too. Who does your hair? I love the highlights."

Mi put a hand up to her hair. "Oh, they're natural."

"That's it. The friendship is off. You cannot have prettier hair than me. I won't allow it."

"Yeah, but look at your legs, they go up to my chin. I'd love to be tall and long legged like you."

"Okay, friendship's back on." Elisa moved to the patio door. "Let's go see if there's anything left of Lucas. Poor boy."

Mi followed her back through the house. Elisa stopped at a table and opened a drawer, pulling out breath mints and a small bottle of perfume. She popped a couple of mints, offering the tin to Mi, then gave herself a spritz of perfume. "Ssh, I'm a secret smoker."

"I won't tell."

"Goes with being the gad-about youngest daughter. I'm only a year and a half older than Lucas, but mentally he's at least ten years older. *Abuelo* made an old man out of him. In a way I feel sorry for Lucas, being the only boy under *Abuelo's* constant scrutiny. He was a... hard man. So cold. He didn't have any use for me, thank God, so he left me alone."

They stopped at the doors to the Rose Room. Elisa put her ear to the panel. "I don't think she's done with him yet," she whispered.

Carla appeared. "Dinner's ready, Miss Vega. Would you like me to announce?"

Elisa waved a hand. "No, thank you, Carla. I'll do it." She waited for Carla to leave. "Watch this," she said to Mi, then threw the doors open dramatically. "Dinner is served," she announced in a heavy British accent, finishing with a deep bow.

"Elisa Maria Guadalupe Vega!" their mother gasped out. "You were raised better than that."

"Sorry, *Mami*." Elisa didn't sound very sorry.

Mi met Lucas's gaze. He held out his hand to her. She went to his side, noting the sharp look his grandmother gave her. Mi guessed Lucas hadn't been successful at bringing her around to Mi's side. He tucked her hand in the crook of his arm and led her into the dining room, leaving his family to follow in their wake.

He leaned down so Mi could hear him. "Are you all right?"

"I am. Are you?"

"I'm really sorry. I wasn't expecting this reaction. She's not normally like this, so... insistent. And rude."

Mi waved off his comment even though she had felt the sting of his grandmother's disapproval quite keenly. "She loves you."

He gave her a pirate's grin that sent a delicious flush of heat straight through her. "I'll make it up to you later."

The dining room was unbelievable, like something off a movie set for a nighttime soap opera. More glitter and sparkle to reflect the light that illuminated several portraits along the walls. Lucas directed Mi to a seat next to the one he took at the head of the table. He waited for everyone to sit before being seated himself.

Mi's eye was drawn to the portrait on the wall directly behind Lucas's chair. It was a full body portrait of a man in his mid-forties dressed in clothing from another era. The hair was in a style of the same time, but the face! Mi's gaze bounced from the portrait to Lucas and back again. The resemblance was striking, so much so that goose bumps scattered over Mi's skin and a chill raced up her spine. The face was the same, and yet not.

"My late husband, Joaquin Vega," Lucas's grandmother said. "God rest his soul." She crossed herself and kissed her locket. She beamed at Lucas with a grandmother's pride. "My grandson is his image, don't you think? He'll carry on the Vega legacy." She pinned Mi with her sharp gaze. "Family is all there is."

Mi found herself agreeing with the older woman. Family was important. What Mi had done, what she continued to do for her own family, was not all that dissimilar to what this grandmother wanted for her only grandson. Mi nodded along. "Family is very important to me, too."

"Then we're in agreement." Lucas's grandmother turned away from Mi as if dismissing her and fixed her stare on her grandson. "Carmen will set aside time this week to bring you up to date with the business. She's done an adequate job, but now that you're home and healed, it's time you took over." She sliced a bite off her steak and looked down the table at Lucas's sister. "Carmen, you will have Mr. Cervantes prepare the necessary paperwork for the transfer to Lucas."

Carmen bowed her head, clearly unhappy about being swept aside by her brother. "Yes, *Abuelita*."

"Don't bother, Carmen. I won't be able to make that appointment." Lucas put a bite of steak in his mouth and chewed, seemingly unaffected by his grandmother's machinations, but Mi knew better. The strain weighed on him. She could see it in the set of his shoulders and how he rubbed his thigh under the table. Her heart went out to him. She reached out for him and stilled his hand, gripping it in her own.

Lucas's mother pushed her food around her plate, looking like she hoped the floor would rise up and swallow her. Elisa went about eating her dinner completely unfazed by what was happening around her. Carmen gave Lucas an unhappy look laced heavily with unmistakable envy.

"You were raised to lead this family and our business," his grandmother pressed on, her tone turning ugly. "Does honor and duty mean nothing to you?"

"You have no idea what honor and duty mean to me. As a soldier, men, good men, lived and *died* everyday around me bound by nothing more than honor and duty." He lowered his voice so that only those sitting next to him—Mi and his grandmother—could hear. "Be very careful about how far you pursue this, *Abuelita*."

The older woman sucked in a breath, then spoke low in rapid-fire Spanish, her tiny hand clamped to Lucas's forearm.

Mi's gaze went again to the portrait. Was this the legacy the old man had intended for his family? The astonishing likeness hit her anew. This was what Lucas would look like in middle age. Already threads of gray wove through his dark hair. The lines of a life well lived were only just beginning to show on Lucas and would only etch deeper as the years passed. As Mi studied the portrait more intently she could easily pick out the differences between Lucas and his grandfather.

Lucas's face reflected a humanity and a resilience the portrait's lacked. The lines in the portrait's face had taken completely different tracks than Lucas's had, having been carved—Mi suspected—by cruelty. The look in the eyes told her as much. And then Lucas's words came back to her: *The day they put* Abuelo *in the ground was one of the happiest days of my life.* What had Elisa said about this man? *He was a... hard man. So cold.*

Mi bit her lip and stared at her untouched plate. Lucas had responsibilities Mi could never be a part of. He'd been groomed to take over as head of the family and business, and to carry on the Vega name with a woman who was a part of his culture, his heritage. Whatever tiny fantasies Mi might have harbored for a future with Lucas died a swift, brutal death. Maybe it was just as well. Her family life was no less complicated, no less of an obligation than his. Their lives were as mismatched as her thrift store dishes and the Vega fine china set on the same table.

Mi pulled her hand from Lucas's, ignoring his quick glance at her, and went through the motions of eating her dinner. For all she could taste, the food might have been made of sawdust and glue. She kept her head down and her mouth shut.

Lucas spat out a few curt sentences to his grandmother in Spanish, ending her rant. Mi could feel the older woman's gaze boring into the top of her head. Whatever Lucas had said to his grandmother sent a rippling of surprise through the other diners. Four heads swiveled at once in her direction. Mi caught Elisa's smile and nod of approval for Lucas. Then, bless her, Elisa launched into detail about her upcoming trip to Europe, stealing everyone's attention.

THE CONVERSATION FLOWED in a new direction, but Lucas found himself unable to focus. He'd made a terrible mistake in bringing Mi here. It seemed as though *Abuelita* was determined to pick up where her husband had left off. She'd made it clear that now that Lucas had been released from the Navy and Vanessa, her mission would be to mold him into the image of his grandfather. But *Abuelita* was not the tyrant her husband had been and Lucas was no longer the boy who couldn't fight back against a man who'd used his strength and size as weapon.

Mi's silence worried him. He could handle whatever

his family threw at him. After all, he'd learned to cope at the hands of a man who made his drill sergeant look like a Kindergarten teacher. Mi didn't deserve the treatment she'd received from his family. So he'd put his foot down. Hard. He hadn't meant to say those things to *Abuelita*, hadn't even known they were in his head. But now that they were out, he couldn't put the ideas away. And maybe he didn't want to.

He put his hand on Mi's knee, needing that small contact. She glanced at him in surprise, then shifted in her chair so that his hand fell away. As soon as dinner was over they'd leave. He'd apologize for his family and try to explain.

He looked down the table, catching Elisa's eye. She flashed him a thumbs-up, giving her approval of Mi, and then she puckered her lips and fluttered her eyelashes, making fun of him. He surreptitiously flipped her the bird. She flashed him a grin in return. God, he'd missed Elisa when he was on deployment. Despite the changes in *Abuelita*, it really was good to be home.

LUCAS GAVE Mi the silence she seemed to need on the drive home. He struggled with the worry that the things *Abuelita* had said, her rudeness, had changed something between him and Mi. She'd barely spoken all evening. And now she sat next to him in the truck, stiff and withdrawn, arms crossed over her chest, legs pressed together much like the way she'd been with him when they'd first met. He hated seeing her like that. Hated that because of him she'd closed up, having gone back into exile within herself.

A sharp pain sliced through his chest, seizing the breath in his lungs. He gripped the wheel harder, trying get a handle on it. The pain morphed to a fist-like ache and then he recognized it for what it was—fear. He wiped the sweat from his upper lip and stole a glance at Mi. She sat unchanged, unaware of his turmoil, staring out into the night. The fear clawed at him, carving hollows in his resolve. He wouldn't be able to make this up to her. He wouldn't get her back.

She'd looked at the portrait of *Abuelo*, listened to his family's talk of legacy and inheritance and came to the same conclusion everyone else did. He was the man his grandfather had made him to be. All of his efforts to fight against it were wasted. He should just take over the company, run it with the same ruthless calculation that flowed from *Abuelo's* blood through to his. He'd take a wife with the proper lineage and breeding. Have sons who he'd mold and shape into his image and continue the legacy *Abuelo* had imagined.

His flight from *Abuelo's* house to the Navy had been a wasted endeavor. Trying to remake himself under the military's thumb had been a futile effort. He'd only exchanged one tyrant for a host of others, one mindset for one that was not all that dissimilar. Why was he fighting it? It would be so much simpler to give in, to allow *Abuelo's* lessons to take hold, be the man he was bred to be.

Dread rode him hard, and he couldn't round up his thoughts on the way home or during the tense, silent elevator ride up to his apartment. And then the doors opened and they stepped into the living room, surrounded by the things of Mi's he'd brought here. It seemed like another time, another place that he'd done this. A time when he could reach out and touch the man he wanted to be, could try that costume on and almost feel like maybe he *was* that man, if only for a little while.

And then he looked at Mi and saw he'd been that man with her. And it wasn't the caricature he'd assumed it was. It was real. He took a hold of her arms, bringing her around to face him fully. He wanted her to really look at him. Wanted her to tell him what she saw when she looked at him. Wanted know if there was any chance he was the kind of man she'd want, the kind of man she could need.

But she stared up at him with huge, blank eyes as though the part of her that had laughed and teased, loved and fought with him had died. A new kind of terror struck him, bringing with it anger and an eerie out of body calm.

"He beat me." The words were out before he could call them back. Not that he would. He had nothing to lose. No reason to care. "I was made to kneel for hours at the side of his desk while he worked. If I moved he hit me. If *Abuelita* or my mother tried to intervene he hit me."

His breath came in harsh bursts and he knew his fingers dug too deep, but he couldn't let her go, couldn't stop now that he'd started. "He used his power and size as a weapon to hurt and intimidate. He wielded it often and mercilessly. He was a monster. And he made me one, too. I laughed."

HIS VOICE CRACKED, his big body shaking so hard that Mi trembled with him. For the first time, she was afraid of him and afraid for him.

"Are you listening?" he shouted, leaning closer to her face, shaking her. "I stood over my grandfather's casket, laughing, and wished him to hell." He released her, pushing her away from him.

She resisted the urge to rub her arms where his fingers had been. Not because he'd hurt her, but because his touch was like fire, burning down all of her defenses. He'd split himself wide for her, opened wounds long since crusted over. She feared she'd never be able to walk away from him.

"That doesn't make you a monster like him. It makes you honest."

"He'd use his belt. The sound of it sliding through his belt loops..." He paused, swallowed. "I can still hear it. The whoosh of it slicing the air above me. And the crack... the crack of it... striking flesh."

He stood in front of her, his body taut as a bowstring. She hurt for him, every part of her ached. His pain was so raw, so real she could almost reach out and touch it, like a live wire, dancing and sparking in the air between them.

"I have his name," he spat like a curse. "His size. For fuck's sake, Mi, I look *exactly* like him."

"But you're not him." She took a risk, laying a hand on

his chest, hoping to impress upon him this point if no other. "You aren't anything like him. Not at all."

"I should never have brought you to that house. In that house he's considered a saint. A god. They want him back. They want me to be him. I didn't know that. I didn't know they'd expect that. I'm so *sorry*."

He stared at her with haunted eyes and she could see the boy he had been deep within their depths. She wanted to weep for him, to hold him to her and rock him and tell him it would all be okay. But she sensed what he needed was to talk, to get it all out. So she stood there and let him, her heart breaking with every word. He turned away from her to look out at the skyline. Her hand fell away, back down to her side. She stayed where she was, her eyes burning with unshed tears.

"I finally got big enough to fight back, but I couldn't." He lifted his hands in a helpless gesture. "It just wasn't in me. That only pissed him off more. He hit harder, trying to goad me into taking a swing at him. Said I wasn't a man if I didn't fight back."

He turned then and everything about him cried defeat. Mi fisted her hands at her sides to keep from going to him and touching him again. Misery flowed off him, vibrating into her in waves that threatened to rise up and swallow them both.

"The last time he beat me, he did it with his fists." He looked away as though the memories played out in front of him, like a flickering old movie. "I was eighteen." He flinched as if they'd delivered a blow. "The next day, bloody and bruised, I enlisted in the Navy. That pissed him off more than my not fighting back."

"Because that's not who you are. He couldn't make you him. He tried and he failed. And then he died." She went to him and wrapped her arms around him, finally able to give him the comfort they both needed. "You're not him. You're not anything like him. He failed." The tears came then, hot and angry at a man she'd never known. She soaked his shirt with them.

"You don't get it," he said miserably.

Standing up on tiptoes, she reached up to put her hands on his face so he'd hear her, really hear her. "He failed, Lucas. He died knowing he failed. No punch you could have delivered would have hurt him as much. Know that. Know that I admire you." She brought him down to her for a kiss. "Know that he never had a hold over you." She kissed him again. "Know that you are a better man than he could ever have hoped to be."

Lucas met her this time, kissing her and holding her with a desperation born of hope. It burst through him like the sun through dark clouds, flooding places inside him so dark he'd forgotten they were there. He ran his hands over her, needing her more than he'd ever needed anything. And the wanting. Aw, fuck the wanting. He couldn't trust himself not to be rough, couldn't trust himself to go slow.

"*Querida*, no." He set her away from him, shaking with the need and the want. "I can't. I won't be gentle. I have to be in you so bad." His hands came up, fisting in his hair, his eyes wide and panicked. "I can't control—"

"I promised you I'd tell you if you ever hurt me."

She stepped back a few paces and pulled her blouse over her head. Aw, fuck— she wasn't wearing a bra. He stilled, staring at her like an alcoholic in front of an open bottle. She slid out of her sandals, dropped her skirt to the floor and kicked it away. With each item she removed, the want rose until he thought he'd drown in it.

"I'm right here," she said, opening her arms. She stood before him in nothing but her panties and the want threatened to spill over.

"You won't hurt me, Lucas," she said, taking a step toward him. "I know you. You could never hurt me. Remember, it's not in you. He's not in you."

He stared at her, swaying.

"Take off your shirt," she ordered. He complied with slow stilted movements. "Now your pants, shoes, all of it."

Finally he was naked before her. A chill raced over his skin though he wasn't cold. And then she bent forward, testing his limits, and slowly peeled her panties down her legs. She threw them, hitting him square in the face. He caught them and blinked at her, balling them in his hand. He almost laughed, the hysteria of the moment close to the limit of what he could bear. She took a step forward, then another. Their bodies brushed. He shuddered.

"I want your hands on me." She twisted slightly, her hardened nipples sweeping across his stomach. "I want your mouth on me." She did it again. "I want you buried deep inside me." And yet again.

He let out a low groan and reached for her with an unsteady hand, unable to help himself. Her skin was petal soft, smelling of flowers. He bent over her, inhaling her scent, pressing her carefully against him. As long as he lived he'd remember the feel of her skin against his. She pushed on his shoulders. He dropped to his knees, then she did, too. She pushed down on him again and his mind finally wrapped around what she wanted. He laid down on the floor with her kneeling over him.

"Condom?"

He blinked up at her, the word drowned out by the pounding of his heart. Then it sank in. He fumbled with his pants and came up with a foil packet, handing it to her. She unwrapped it and slowly rolled it on. He watched her, thinking any moment he'd break apart. His control would snap and the monster would come out.

She sat back on her heels and studied him a moment. "You have to do it. You have to prove to yourself that you can. Make love to me, Lucas, and don't hold back."

She kissed him lightly on the lips, then sat back again. Their gazes locked, she dipped a hand between her legs and stroked, her other hand going to her breast. He watched, mesmerized, as she pleasured herself. Her head fell back and a soft sigh slipped from her lips. Before he knew what he meant to do, he was on her, pressing her back to the floor, wedging himself between her legs. He thrust into her all at once. She gasped, arching into him. He rocked into her again. She didn't stop him.

Something basic and primal took over as he pounded into her, grunting with the effort. There was no finesse, no technique. Just the harsh sound of flesh slapping flesh and her cries of encouragement, driving him on. All thought fled. It was just him and her and the want over-riding it all. He burst, pouring into her with a roar wrenched from deep inside. He collapsed in a heap on top of her, gasping for breath.

She murmured something that got drowned out by the blood rushing in his head. Somewhere in the back of his mind he snagged a piece of it, the intent behind the words, and then quickly hid it away, afraid to believe, afraid it was only the moment, the sex that had forced them out of her.

He rolled off her, coming to rest on the floor beside her. Lying on their backs, they stared up at the ceiling side by side. She took his hand.

It was a miracle. She was a miracle. That she would accept him, knowing all that she knew about him. He felt like he should say something. Words of gratitude, of how she made him feel, or how much she meant to him.

But no words came.

HE LAY with her in bed later that night, playing with the fringes of sleep. She snored, a little rasping sound, but he didn't mind. The sound of her, the weight of her against his body, the smell of her, warm and feminine, her hair tickling his chest, felt right. All of it. They'd finished not that long ago, but he wanted her again. He wondered when or if that constant craving would lessen. Wondered if she felt the same. He brushed his fingers over the curve where her ass met her legs. She stirred, shifting her leg over his, opening for him.

He thought for a moment she had woken up, but her snoring continued uninterrupted. And then it occurred to him how every time he reached for her she was there, ready and willing. He didn't know what he'd done to deserve her or even why she'd want him. But she did.

He rolled her gently to her back. She sighed, turning her head to the side, and settled more firmly into the pillows. The cat leapt onto the bed and snuggled into the curve of her neck. Still she didn't move. Her skin glowed in the moonlight as though she'd been bathed in moon dust. The sheet over her had slipped, revealing one breast. He should resist, let her sleep. Intending to do just that, he bent down and kissed the slope of her breast as a goodnight.

"You keep that up, you're going to have to finish what you started."

Startled, he looked up at her and grinned. "You want me to start something?"

"Like you need encouragement."

"I'll take all the encouragement I can get."

"Hmm. I bet." Reaching up, she stretched, and the other breast popped free of the sheet. The cat complained loudly and jumped off the bed.

"You're encouraging me, *querida*."

"Am I? I thought I was stretching." She did it again, arching her back, all but waving her breasts in his face.

Growling, he slipped his arms under her, practically serving her up for his attentions. He circled her nipples with hot, opened mouthed kisses, first one breast then the other. Gripping the headboard, she let out a purr of approval, definitely encouraging him. Laying his tongue out flat, he slowly licked the underside of her breast, up and over her nipple. She gasped, grinding her pelvis against the leg he'd wedged between hers. He paid the other side the same attention, adding a swirl over the nipple.

"Oh, God you're good at that," she panted.

He kissed her, his mouth hot and hungry over hers, showing her with his lips and tongue how he'd love her. He broke the kiss, tracing the line of her shoulder to her neck with little nips of his teeth. She writhed against him, using her hands and mouth, devastating his intentions to pleasure only her.

"*Querida*," he whispered, his lips trailing down her neck.

"Hmm?" She wrapped her clever little fingers around his cock, doing that thing she did with her other hand and he forgot his name, forgot to breathe as she stroked him.

He reached past her, fumbling in the nightstand drawer, and finally came up with his prize. Taking her nipple in his mouth, he rasped his tongue over the sensitive tip and her hands fell away from him to grip his head, fastening him to her. Slipping a finger into her, he tested her readiness. She pushed her pelvis up, driving his finger deeper, then flexed down and up once again. Tipping her head back, she moaned in pre-orgasmic bliss.

He broke free of her breast and stared down at her in amazement, his breath ragged. "I'm never going enough of you, you know that?"

"God, I hope not," she said, bringing him down for a kiss.

Blindly he secured the condom and reached for her

again. She twisted out from under him and turned, presenting him with her backside. He gripped her hips, kneading the flesh there. She looked over her shoulder at him, her cheeks flushed, her eyes heavy with desire and wiggled her ass against his dick. He groaned and positioned himself at her entrance. He slid in slowly with her backing up to meet him.

She fisted the sheet and let out a low moan. He slid almost all the way out then back in again, holding her hips so he had control. She tried to set the speed, but he held her firmly, communicating that he was in charge and she'd just have to take it as he gave it. Then he continued his slow torture, never quite giving her the pace she wanted. Smoothing his hands up her sides and around to the front, he held her breasts in his hands. Playing with her nipples in time with his strokes, he drove her higher until she was begging for release.

Sweat beaded his brow from the effort of withholding and he thought for a moment he'd die from it. And then she clamped a hand on the headboard, setting something off inside him. He clasped her hips and drove into her over and over, faster and faster. She convulsed around him. He thrust once, twice, and leaned over her, twining his fingers with hers on the headboard as he too found his pleasure, driving deep.

He withdrew from her reluctantly, giving her a playful swat on the bottom, then kissed the sting. She moaned and flopped flat on her stomach. He left to dispose of the condom and came back to discover her snoring softly, still face down. Chuckling, he climbed into bed and drew the covers over her, tucking them around her.

The words he couldn't find earlier came to him then, filling his head in big neon letters. Rolling to look at her, they blazed brighter. He reached out and touched her cheek, needing the contact. He kissed her shoulder, whispering the words against her skin first in Spanish, then in English.

"*Te amo*. I love you, *querida*."

CHAPTER 4

"Thank you, detective." Mi clicked her phone closed and gnawed on her lip. She'd woken up early the next morning to call Detective Rolls for news on Tracey. There was still no sign of her. According to Rolls, her disappearance combined with something the police had found in her phone records made her a "person of interest" in the studio bombing.

Lucas came into the living room fresh from the shower, wearing nothing but a pair of faded, low-slung jeans, his hair damp and curling around his neck and ears. Her girl parts took notice, her nipples hardening against her t-shirt, her panties suddenly damp. Realizing her jaw hung open, she shut it with a snap. It was like he'd flipped some kind of switch inside her, tuning her to Lucas mode, causing her body to automatically react every time he came near.

"Something wrong?" he asked.

She flashed him her phone. "Detective Rolls called. There's no sign of Tracey. It's like she just vanished."

"And?"

"He's getting a warrant to search her apartment."

"They think she had something to do with the bombing."

He dropped the statement like a water balloon, splashing her with anger. It was one thing to hear it from Detective Rolls and quite another to know that Lucas would jump straight to that conclusion without at least trying to give her friend the benefit of doubt.

"Do *you*?" she snapped back.

He put his hands up like two big, meaty stop signs. "That's for the police to decide. Not me."

She stood up, propping her hands on her hips. "Really? Because it sounded like you believe she could have done it. Davy died! You really think someone who I considered a friend would commit murder? What does that say about your opinion of me and my judgment?"

"*Querida,* you're tired. Overstressed."

She knew he was right, but damn it. Why couldn't he just placate her and stamp out the rampant doubts that had been playing at the back of her mind about Tracey instead of encouraging them? She *was* tired and over-stressed, but hearing him call her that tipped her over to flat out pissed off.

"So my judgment's impaired then, is that what you're saying?" She folded her arms across her chest and flung herself head-long down a road she knew she shouldn't go with him. "Because if that's the case, then maybe I'm off about a whole bunch of other things as well."

He eyed her carefully. She supposed a man with three

sisters knew a female minefield when he saw one. "That's not what I meant."

"Then what *did* you mean?"

"I really hope your friend isn't involved."

She threw up her hands. "Why didn't you just say that?"

He looked like he'd answer, then shook his head.

Her cell phone rang. She looked down at the caller ID, then stomped off down the hall to the bedroom half expecting him to follow her. She turned to close the bedroom door and caught sight of him shaking his head, mumbling something to himself.

She flipped her phone open. "Hi, Mom."

"Miyuki?"

She sat down on the couch at the end of the bed. "Yes, it's me."

"Oh. I was trying to call your Aunt Betty. She was supposed to come over and watch Ethan so I could go to the grocery store."

Mi popped off the couch. "Mom, Aunt Betty passed away four years ago, remember?"

"No, that was Uncle Eric."

Closing her eyes, she squeezed her forehead between her thumb and fingers. Jason's dad was named Eric and as far as anyone knew he wasn't dead. "What do you need from the store?"

"Store?"

"You said you needed to go to the store."

"I don't know..." There was a long pause, then, "I had to put him in the fire. The fire purges. The fire cleanses. He wasn't clean. I made him clean."

Mi paced to the far side of the room, her insides cramping. "Mom. What fire?"

"Why are you yelling?"

"I'm not." She tried to keep her voice calm, but it wobbled. "Where is the fire, Mom?"

There was a loud commotion in the background, a splitting sound followed by shouting.

"Get out of my house!" her mother shrieked.

"Mom!"

More yelling, then her mom's voice somewhere in the distance, tinny and frightened. "Miyuki. Miyu..." The line went dead.

Mi pulled her phone away from her ear and shouted into it. "Mom! Mom!" Over and over she cried until Lucas burst into the room.

"What's wrong?"

She stared up at him, the phone clutched in her hand. He took it from her and put it to his ear, then snapped it shut.

"What's going on?" he demanded.

"We have to go. We have to go." She ran to the closet, grabbed her shoes and headed to the elevator with Lucas on her heels.

He gripped her elbow and pulled her around. "What's going on? Where are you going?"

She jerked her arm out of his grasp and punched the call button for the elevator, then punched it again.

"Mi, wait," he told her, then jogged back down the hall.

"Come on, come on." She smacked the button over

and over until the doors finally slid open. She jumped inside and hit the lobby button.

Lucas slid into the elevator, a shirt and gun in one hand, shoes and keys in the other. "What's going on? Where are we going?"

She paced the small space, fear squeezing her insides like a garlic press. Fire. Shit. Not again. Shit. Shit. Shit. She exploded out of the elevator, Lucas right on her heels.

He pulled her up short just before she hit the door to the garage. "We're not going one more step until you tell me what's going on." She tried to jerk away, but he only hauled her in closer. "*Querida.*"

"My mom put Ethan in the fire again. I have to go."

"*What?*"

"Lucas, please. Please. We have to go."

He didn't argue. Didn't ask any more questions. It occurred to her vaguely that she should have wondered about that, but panic rode her hard and she couldn't think about anything except getting to her mom.

While they waited in his truck for the garage gate to roll up, he looked over at her. She could see the concern etched into the space between his brows. Why didn't that gate move faster?

"Where are we going?" he asked, slipping his shirt over his head.

"My mom's house in Garland." She pounded the dashboard. "Hurry up, you stupid gate."

They didn't speak until they were on the freeway. Lucas had managed to put his shoes on at stoplights, but they weren't tied. The occasional worried looks he cast her only intensified her frustration and dread until she couldn't take it anymore.

She turned to the window so she wouldn't have to see his reaction to what she was about to tell him. He would look at her differently, as though she carried her mother's madness just under the surface. There were times when she was sure she did. Like some dormant virus, it lay in wait for the perfect storm of contentment and happiness in her life to flood her system. Just like her mother.

She tried to remember a time when her mother was normal, but the last thirteen years had coated those memories over with a fine layer of dusty soot and misery. Like photos stored too long in an attic, the images of her life "before" were pale with grime and hardly worth looking at. They were filled with people who didn't exist anymore and places in her heart she'd never get to revisit.

"My mother is... different," she began, then quickly backtracked, frustrated with herself. "Remember you asked me if I had a baby when we first met?" She didn't give him a chance to answer. "I don't. My mom did. A boy, Ethan. He... died. My mom didn't... take it well."

She paused, uncertain how to explain the next part. Everything she came up with sounded, well, crazy. He didn't speak and she could only be grateful to him for it. She was awash with gratitude toward him, she realized sickly, and wondered if she'd confused real affection for massive indebtedness. Maybe they were too tightly woven to be separated. She'd have to think about that later, trace the strands to see which was the strongest.

She took a breath and dove in again. "I found something that helped her. Shit." She put up a hand. "Please don't say anything when I'm done. Promise me I won't have to talk about this again. And no questions."

"Why would you ask me to make a promise if you don't expect me to keep it?"

She looked at him then, her eyes wide with shock. Did he really know her that well? He glanced at her, taking his eyes off the road long enough so she could see the depth of his loyalty. She stacked it with the other things she was grateful to him for and turned her attention back to the window.

"A doll." God, this sounded so stupid. "I got a doll and dressed it in Ethan's clothes. She *takes care* of it. Pretends it's Ethan. The car seat, baby bed, all of it is to keep the illusion going. Keep her... stable. But sometimes... sometimes it doesn't work."

Rocking a little in her seat, she hugged herself, biting her lip. This is where the questions would come: Why didn't they ever get her mother psychiatric help? What about medication? Should she be hospitalized? Is she a danger to herself or others? How often do these things happen?

But he remained silent, leaning over to capture her hand and giving it a squeeze. She squeezed back, keeping her gaze on the passing cars. She appreciated the support, but knew it wouldn't last. She'd only opened one of the doors of her past. The other one well... that was where the real nightmare lurked. He wasn't asking questions now, but he would. And when he did, it would change things between them forever.

She directed him off the freeway to her mother's house. They turned the corner onto her street and found emergency vehicles blocking the way. As soon as Lucas pulled to the side of the road, Mi leapt from the truck and ran to her mother's house. It took her a few terror-filled moments to locate her mother on the porch of the neighbor's house. When she saw her mom safe, she nearly sank to her knees with relief.

Lucas jogged up behind her and spun her around. "Don't ever fucking run off like that again."

"What?"

Anger darkened his features, turning his eyes black and his lips into a thin hard line. If he was imposing before, he was downright terrifying when furious. "You took off without me."

"Miyuki?" her mother called from the neighbor's porch.

"I lost sight of you when you went behind the fire truck," he snapped.

Out of the corner of her eye, she could see her mother stepping off the porch and she cringed inside.

"Miyuki?" her mother called again.

LUCAS TURNED toward the voice calling Mi's name. A blond woman about the right age to be Mi's mother walked toward them, clutching a blue baby blanket. Mi seemed to wither away, her gaze darting back and forth between the woman and him as though she'd been caught doing something she shouldn't.

He could tell the woman had been beautiful in her youth, but her face had been gouged deep by the hard edges of life. She'd made a valiant effort to recapture her looks with makeup, but had overdone it, reminding Lucas of a paint-by-numbers portrait. Red lipstick bled into the creases around her mouth and when she kissed Mi on the cheek she left a stain, like a lonely lip print on an empty shot glass.

He stood to the side while the two women exchanged greetings, wondering how in the world these two could possibly be related. Mi was petite, at least a head shorter than her mother, and dark where her mother was light. He couldn't find a single point of similarity between them. Not one single feature matched in shape, size or color. And then the older woman turned to him and he saw it—that same deep unfathomable kindness in her eyes as in Mi's. He found himself liking her even before he knew her.

"Mom, this is Lucas Vega. Lucas, my mom, Faye Easley," Mi said.

Lucas held out his hand. "Pleased to meet you, Ms. Easley."

She gave his hand a firm shake. "Nice to meet you, too." She took her hand back and clutched the blanket to her chest, then turned to Mi. "Where have you been? You're late. Is he why you're late?"

"No, Mom. What happened?"

"You know you're not old enough to date. Is he a senior? He looks like a senior."

"Where's Mrs. Crandall?"

"Oh, Miyuki." Tears welled in Ms. Easley's eyes. She wrung the blanket like a dirty dishrag.

Lucas took a step back as Mi wrapped an arm around

her mother's shoulders, closing him out of their conversation. He'd been so focused on Mi and the people around them that hadn't glanced at the house. It would be a total loss. The windows were black eyes that once looked out onto a nice neighborhood, a few steps up from Mi's. A fact that irritated him at the same time it impressed him —she would give her mother better than she gave herself. He now understood where all her money went— to this house and to take care of her mother.

Part of the house's roof had caved in. There would be water damage. He watched the firemen wind up their hoses and put their equipment away by rote. Her mother was lucky to have gotten out unharmed. She wouldn't be able to stay here anymore. He wondered if Mi had a backup plan. Knowing what he knew of her finances, he'd bet not.

So much made sense now: Mi's lack of funds, her unwillingness to talk about her family, the stuff with her brother, the secret phone calls. There was more to the story, he was sure. She'd picked her way through telling it. Frowning, he studied Mi's body language as she spoke quietly with her mother. Did she really think he wouldn't understand? After spending one evening with his family, she'd have to know that he would. Whatever secrets she kept, she held onto them as tightly as her mother did that blanket. He'd put money down on it having something to do with her baby brother's death.

He'd held off grilling her for more details, but her respite would be temporary. As soon as he got her back home, they would sit down and talk. She had been right not to expect him to make that promise.

He should be angry with her, but he wasn't. He understood her now. She'd been through so much, lost so much. He was just so damn glad her mother was okay. That, at least, wouldn't be added to the list of all the fucking awful things she'd been through lately. He surveyed the ruins of the house, another significant loss. His gaze tracked back to Mi and he caught her looking at him. There was a wariness in her expression that punched a hole in his gut. And pissed him off.

She glanced away and bit into her lower lip. Fuck it all. He'd give anything to make sure she never did that again. He took a step toward her at the same time one of the firemen approached her and her mother. Joining the group, he caught the most salient information.

"—uninhabitable. I'm sorry for your loss."

Mi sighed. "Thank you, captain."

"I can stay with Vicky—" her mother started to say.

"No, Mom. Let me call Jason." Mi took out her cell phone and dialed. "Hey, um... there's been a little accident at Mom's house. Yeah, she's okay. I know. Would you just *stop*?" She listened, her small body vibrating like a plucked spring. "She needs a place to stay." She huffed out a breath. "I don't know how long. No. I just can't right now." She groaned, stepping into the shade of the neighbor's house, away from her mother. Lucas followed.

"Jas, *please*," Mi pleaded.

While Mi begged her brother to take their mother in, Lucas studied her. Her lower lip trembled slightly, her gaze fixed to a point in the distance, and she gripped the phone as though it was the only thing tethering her to the earth. She hadn't asked for his help, stubborn woman. Instead she turned to her useless piece of shit brother. He'd better come through for her, Lucas thought.

She sagged a shoulder against the house, clicking her phone shut. "He says she can stay with him for a few days, but after that I have to find her someplace else to live."

"She can stay with us," he offered without thinking.

"No."

"Why not?"

"Just no." She looked out to where her mother stood by a fire truck, smoothing the blanket over her cheek. "This is not your problem."

Feeling his shoulders tighten with annoyance, he shoved his hands in his pockets. "Why won't you let me help you?"

"I told you, it's not your problem."

"What if I want to make it my problem?"

Her gazed whipped to his, her eyes red rimmed and sharp with anger. "Let it go."

"You don't make it easy to care for you."

"We're just fuck buddies, remember?"

Fury roared through him like a wild fire, his voice taking on a quiet menace he couldn't control. "Just fuck buddies, huh?" He edged toward her. She backed away into a corner between some bushes and the house where they couldn't be seen from the street. Lifting her, he brought his leg up between hers, pinning her to the wall with his body. He kissed her hard, rubbing her mound against his leg. He slipped a hand under the hem of her shirt to her breast. And just like that she responded.

Holding on to his shoulders, she gave back as good as

she got. Rolling her nipple between his fingers, he kissed her neck just below her jaw where he knew it drove her crazy. Tipping her head back, she let out a soft cry and gripped him harder. Riding his leg, she panted, the beginnings of her orgasm taking control of her body. He could make her come right here, didn't even have to get her naked.

Then suddenly he released her, his breath coming in harsh puffs. "We're more than fuck buddies, *querida*." Taking in her red swollen lips, heavy lidded gaze, and the rapid rise and fall of her breasts, he wanted her now and forever. Did she really not know that? He bent low and pressed his forehead to hers, looking into her eyes so she could see. "So much more," he whispered and then he kissed her softly, pouring everything he wanted to say into that one kiss.

She melted into him, twining her arms around his neck. He broke the kiss and held her, stroking her hair. She sighed deeply, her breath hot on his chest.

"Let me help you," he said.

"Lucas, please."

Aw, fuck. Now she was begging him just like she did her useless piece of shit brother. "All right. I won't push. But I'm here if you need anything, okay?"

She nodded against his chest. "Thank you."

He tilted her face up to his. "Anything for you."

MI WOULD HAVE LIKED the luxury of dissecting Lucas's words, trying to decipher the meaning behind them based on his tone and timing, but just then her mother called for her. The panic in her mother's voice jolted Mi back to the torn reality of her life. She broke free from Lucas, feeling guilty for resenting her mother so much.

He put a hand on her arm, stopping her. "I mean it, *querida*. Whatever you need."

She nodded again, gladder than she had any right to be about his offer of help. He released her and fell into step beside her. Always by her side, on her side. She hadn't done anything to deserve him or his loyalty. But she couldn't help but be grateful all the same.

CHAPTER 5

They had to stop at a store to pick up clothes and other things her mother would need now that everything she'd owned was either burned or damaged except for the things in her purse, which she'd managed to grab before fleeing the house. Lucas stood by, his hand practically hovering over his wallet. Mi nearly groaned out loud when the total popped up on the register. She handed over the credit card she'd given her mother, hoping it wouldn't be declined. She sent up a silent prayer laced heavily with guilt. Really, couldn't one damn thing go her way for once? Surely she'd reached some sort of cosmic limit with all of the crappy things she'd been through.

Lucas frowned at her deep sigh of relief as the register printed out the receipt. She could practically hear his brain cells sizzling in frustration. She appreciated his offer of help, she really did, but she just couldn't take any more from him. Her mother was her responsibility. The more involved he got with her mother, the more he'd expect to *be* involved. He'd want answers to the questions Mi so desperately didn't want to answer.

They stopped by Mi's house to pick up a few more items. Mi hadn't been back to her house since the night she left with Lucas. She had expected it to be a mess, especially after the police had gone through it and dusted for fingerprints, but it was clean. So clean she knew in an instant a cleaning crew had been through the house.

Standing in the living room with Lucas while her mother used the bathroom, she rolled her head his direction. "You had my house *cleaned*?"

"Yeah," he said with a one-shoulder shrug.

She put her hands over her face and would've sat down except all there was to sit on was his awful, jagged furniture. Which looked absolutely ridiculous in her house. Just another item on the long list of things Lucas had done for her. She didn't know why she was surprised he'd had her house cleaned, too. She should have expected it.

If she needed to dry her hands he was practically there holding the towel for her. If she felt the slightest twinge of hunger, he was there with a plate of food in his hands. If she could have come up with one thing she'd done for *him* she might not have been so upset. But there was nothing. Unless you counted the sex. Except there again he came out on top, giving her at least two orgasms to his one. Damn it.

"Stop doing stuff like that," she said.

"What?"

"Cleaning my house, bringing my stuff over to your house, helping me take care of my mother, letting me live with you, feeding me all the time, protecting me, giving me more orgasms than I give you."

A corner of his mouth bent up. "Excuse me?"

"You know what I mean."

"I tell you what, I'll let you give me an orgasm as soon as we're alone."

"I'm serious."

"So am I, *querida*." He leaned down and nipped her earlobe. "Very serious," he whispered, sending an illicit chill over her skin.

"I mean it, Lucas."

"I know." He rubbed the sting from her ear lobe between his thumb and finger. "I like doing things for you."

She liked it, too. "But it's not even. You've done way more for me than I've done for you."

"We're keeping score?"

"Well, no. I mean, yes... sort of."

He wrapped his arms around her, bringing her in close. "Then by my score I owe you. Unless we're talking orgasms, in that case you definitely owe me. I'll begin collecting as soon as we get home."

"Deal. But you're wrong about owing me."

"Am I? Let's see... I now have a couch I can take a nap on without damaging vital organs. I have someone to take care of my cat. I now have a job I'm fairly good at. I don't have to eat alone any more. I now know there's another type of bullet that has nothing to do with guns. I'm with someone my sister finally approves of. I have someone in my life who won't fuck her personal trainer on the side and isn't screwing me to get at my money. And my favorite: I'm owed about forty-seven orgasms."

She laughed and it felt so good. "By my calculations I only owe you sixteen."

"Fine. Look, I get that you're independent. I've tried to respect that. But you can't fault me for wanting to do nice things for you."

"I'm not... I'm just not comfortable with how *much* you've done for me."

"How about I take those sixteen orgasms and we call it even?"

She punched him in the shoulder. "Be serious."

He chuckled and rubbed the spot. "Ouch."

"Miyuki!" her mom yelled.

Both of their heads came up and she jumped out of his arms.

"Shit," she muttered and headed down the hall. Halfway there, she turned. "I mean it. Cut it out with all the nice stuff for a while."

"All right," he grumbled. "But as soon as those sixteen orgasms are paid up the moratorium is off."

Insufferable man, she mumbled to herself as she headed down the hall to see her mother. But damn, he could make her laugh and sigh in ecstasy better than any man she'd ever known. She shouldn't think about tomorrow. She shouldn't think past the sixteen orgasms she owed him. Oh, how she wanted to though.

She didn't find her mom in the bathroom. "Mom?" She looked in her room, then the spare bedroom. She finally found Faye hunched down on the floor next to the bassinet, rocking back and forth. "Mom," she whispered, kneeling down next to her. "What's wrong?"

"I can't find Ethan." She grabbed the front of Mi's shirt, pulling Mi toward her. "You did something to him," Faye spat, twisting Mi's shirt in her fist, drawing her off balance. Her blue eyes, dark with anxiety, gave her an almost feral look.

Oh, God. "He's okay. I didn't do anything to him."

"Then the devil has him. I know it." She jerked on Mi's shirt. "Don't lie to me!"

"I'm not, Mom. I swear. He's okay. Nobody's got him."

Mi should have expected it, but Faye was too quick. The crack to the cheek sent Mi against the wall. Her head hit hard and she slid to the floor. Then her mom was on her, pinning Mi's arms down with her legs.

"You were always a terrible liar," Faye hissed, wrapping her hands around Mi's throat. "It's your fault. All of it's your fault."

Mi kicked, trying to buck her mother off, but Faye was bigger, stronger.

"You killed Ronin!" her mother yelled, digging her fingers into her daughter's neck. "I hate you! I hate you!"

In the next instant Mi was freed. She rolled onto her side, facing the wall, gasping and choking. Lucas bent down to her, holding a kicking and screaming Faye around the middle with one arm.

"Mi! Holy shit. Are you all right?" He turned her toward him, his gaze locked on the marks on her throat. "Jesus fucking Christ. I'm calling an ambulance."

She grabbed a hold of his pant leg. "No," she croaked out.

He wrestled Faye to the ground, placing a knee on her back, holding both of her hands in his in a tight grip. "She tried to kill you."

Mi rose up on her elbow, fingering her sore neck. "No ambulance," she wheezed.

"She needs to be locked up, Mi. She tried to *kill* you, for fuck's sake. I don't care if she is your mother, she belongs in jail."

Panic flooded back into Mi's system, making it harder to breathe. Specks floated before her eyes. "No!" she managed. "No police. No." She wrapped her arms around his leg, holding on for all she was worth. "Promise me. No."

"*Querida*," he moaned. "Don't ask this. You're hurt. She *hurt* you."

"I'm fine." She used his leg to haul herself up to sitting and leaned against the wall. "I'll be fine."

He pulled out his cell phone and began dialing.

"No!" She batted it out of his hand. "No police, Lucas. I swear to God if you call the police we are over." She drew back, breathing hard, meaning every word she said. He had no idea what was at stake. She hadn't worked so goddamned hard the last thirteen years to let him fuck it up now. "No police."

He looked at her as if he didn't know her, couldn't believe what she'd become. Her words seemed to freeze him. Behind his stare she could see him weighing the strength of her threat. She held her breath, ready to back up her words with action. Mi's gaze cut to her mom, who quietly sobbed into the carpet, her eyes pinched shut.

Oh, God. Mi made a move to crawl to her mother, but Lucas put a hand up, stopping her.

"Stay the fuck away from her," he snarled.

Mi sat back, and their face-off continued. Dark eyes bored into hers. A sob hiccupped in her throat as the enormity of what had just happened came crashing down around her in big flaming chunks. Her mother had tried to kill her. Jesus. Fuck. She thunked her head against the wall once, twice, trying to dislodge the memory of her mother's face above hers, murder in her eyes.

"Stop that," he commanded.

"She tried to kill me," Mi whispered, the words torn from deep inside her. She covered her face with her hands and broke down, drawing her legs up tight. "She ac-ca-cused me of k-k-killing my dad."

"Fuck me," he breathed, sitting down hard on the floor.

Mi pulled her hands away from her face and glared at her mother. "Why, Mom? Why? Why did you do that? Why do you hate me so much?" Her tears flowed freely, hot and full of shame. "What did I do wrong? What did I ever do?"

Faye stared back from her place on the floor, her gaze empty and searching. Lucas hauled Faye up and marched her out into the hall, leaving Mi's words ringing hollowly in the empty room.

Mi dropped her head onto her knees. It was all so fucked up. Lucas, her mom, her brother, all of the people who mattered. She had nothing and no one. She was alone with her secret.

"*Querida.*" He picked her up and sat on the edge of the bed, cradling her against his chest. She could hear his heart pounding against her cheek. "I don't know what to do. Tell me what to do for you."

She clutched the front of his shirt, bringing his face down to hers. "No police. Promise me."

"Why? You have to tell me why."

"Don't make me chose."

"What the hell are you talking about?"

She pounded a fist ineffectually against his chest. "Promise me."

"Mi—" he began to protest, but stopped when he saw the fierce look on her face. She'd left him no choice. He nodded, his face set in rigid lines. "I promise."

She sagged against him. "Thank you." She pressed a kiss to his hard-set lips. "Thank you."

He set her away from him. "She ever lays a fucking hand on you again…" He let the threat hang in the air between them unsaid, but it was as real as if he'd written it in blood. His gaze dropped to her neck where he lightly traced the marks her mother's hands had made. His brows creased in a deep frown, his jaw ticking from being clenched so tightly.

"Where is she?"

He glanced up, surprised. "I locked her in the closet. Why?"

"*What?*" She tried to scramble off his lap, but he held her fast.

"Stop it."

"I need to see her."

"Hell no." He held her tighter, burrowing his face in her shoulder.

"I have to see if she's okay."

"She's fine. Give it a minute."

She realized he was trembling. This big man who had seen battle quaked as badly as she did. She held onto him, burning with a mixture of shame and regret. Shame for what he'd seen and regret for not being able to choose him above all else.

"I'm so sorry," she whispered, her voice still hoarse. It wasn't enough. She could apologize a thousand times and it would never erase what had happened in this room. It would never be enough. He should run, just go as far as and fast away from her as he could. "Oh, Lucas. I'm so sorry. You deserve better. I can't be what you need. What you deserve."

"Shut up."

"I knew I shouldn't have tried to do this. I just wanted you so much. Even knowing it would end. I don't have any regrets. I hope... please don't hate me. Please know how much I—"

"Shut the fuck up," he growled.

Leaning her back over his arm, he kissed her, sealing her words away. He was rough, kissing her as though he wasn't sure he'd ever get the chance again. She absorbed his heat, his anger, his fear and frustration, wishing it all away. He held the back of her head in his hand, fastening her to him. The other hand crept under her shirt and splayed across her back. She moaned into his mouth, aroused despite the circumstances, but that didn't seem to please him.

He pulled his hand out, parking it on her hip, and broke the kiss. "Damn it." He looked down at her and all she saw was sadness, his dark eyes shining like slick black pools.

"I'm sorry," she said.

"Stop saying that."

"But I am."

"When we get home—"

"Nothing's going to change," she broke in.

"—we're going to sit down and figure this out."

"It's not your problem," she insisted.

He stood up and set her back down on the bed. Fisting his hands in his hair, he paced away, then back again. He stopped and pointed a finger at her. "I don't ever want to hear you say that again. Do you hear me?"

"But it's true."

"The fuck it is."

"Lucas, stop. You can't fix this."

He dropped his hands. "And you can? How's your way working so far? Your *fix* almost got you killed."

Sucking in a breath, she flinched as if he'd hit her. "Screw you."

He dropped to his knees in front of her, gripping her by the shoulders. "Do you know what seeing her on top of you, her hands wrapped around your throat, did to me? Do you?"

"I don't care."

"It fucking scared the shit out of me." He gave her a little shake. "I can't let anything happen to you."

"Why not? What do you care? What does anybody care? My own mother hates me."

"Why do I care?"

She tried to break free from his hold. "Just forget it."

He let her go. "Damn it, Mi. Don't you get it?"

"I said forget it."

He brought her face around to his, made her look him in the eye. "I more than care, *querida*."

Tears spilled over her cheeks. He kissed them, murmuring to her in Spanish. When he'd kissed them all, he put his forehead to hers, smoothing his thumbs over the last of her tears. "Don't you get it, you crazy, sexy, infuriating, beautiful woman? I love you." He laughed as though he'd only just discovered that fact. "I fucking love you. And I don't care if you don't love me back right now. We're going home and we're going to figure this out. Do you hear me?"

He'd stunned her into silence. She could only stare at him, her jaw slack, her heart beating a rhythm that pounded in her ears. What had she done? She could live the rest of her life without him, alone, loving him so much she ached with it. It hadn't ever occurred to her that he could love her back.

If it were only her mom she'd been protecting, she wouldn't bother to do it anymore. Her mother was beyond her help and protection, but there was someone else. Someone who still needed her to keep the secret. Someone who deserved her silence.

So Mi kept quiet when all she wanted to do was scream.

CHAPTER 6

"We can't take her to Jason's," Mi said, casting a wary glance at her mother sitting at the kitchen table, rocking the spare doll Mi had stashed away.

Lucas looked at the older woman and suppressed the urge that rode him hard. He'd never wanted to kill anyone in his life. He'd killed, but he never *wanted* to do it. Never fired his gun, used his hands, or wielded a weapon with the burning desire to end a life. His mind kept flashing images at him of Mi helpless and dying, her mother's hands around her throat, Mi gasping for air, the marks on her neck. And his blood lust simmered.

He got that Mi's mom was mentally ill and he felt bad about that. But he also wanted to call the men in white coats and have her carted away. Faye obviously needed help, possibly medication, but for whatever reason Mi wouldn't allow that. She had been right about the doll calming Faye down. But for how long? How long until she went for Mi or someone else again? What if he wasn't there next time?

"I think she should stay here. She's stayed here before several times and some of... Ethan's things are here for her," Mi said.

As much as he hated Faye Easely for what she'd done to Mi, he couldn't let her stay in Mi's house. "It's not safe here. Gann could come back. What if he used your mother to get to you?"

"Oh, God. I didn't think of that."

"Why can't she go to your brother's?"

She looked at her mother, biting her lip, and all Lucas could think was, *Who the hell is she protecting? Why was she willing to risk their relationship and her* life *to protect them?*

"I guess there's no other choice." She didn't meet his gaze, had hardly looked at him at all since he'd blurted out that he *fucking* loved her.

Way to go, Mr. Romance. Just what a woman wants to hear from a guy right after he stuck his tongue down her throat out of misplaced frustration. As a post near-death experience, his ass-hat attempt at romance was nothing short of brilliant. He'd kick his own ass if it were physically possible. *I fucking love you.* Sheer romantic genius, ya idiot.

"All right, we'll take her to Jason's, but we can't tell him what happened," she said.

He was really getting tired of hearing that. "Why the hell not? What if she goes for him or a neighbor?"

"She won't."

"How can you be sure? This is a bad idea. I should never have agreed not to call the police."

"Look at her. As long as she has the doll she'll be okay."

"And the fire at her house?"

"She won't do that again," she said tightly. "Look, you don't have to be involved."

"Too late for that and I told you, I'm all in here so stop offering me a way out. You're pissing me off."

"Fine. Then we'll take her to Jason's—"

"I know," he interrupted. "Don't worry, I won't tell him that his mother tried to kill his sister."

"Stop it."

"Just hurry up and get her stuff and let's get out of here."

He watched Mi head down the hall, then turned to where her mother sat, singing a lullaby to a fucking doll. Easing down into the seat opposite Faye, Lucas looked at the woman who had given Mi life and who had also nearly taken it away. He wasn't that big of a hard ass that he didn't feel sorry for her. He could manage compassion, for fuck's sake.

It was cruel of Mi and her brother not to get their mother help. He didn't feel bad for thinking that. It *was* cruel. They'd let her illness have her. Left her trapped in a world where the calm of caring for her dead son's substitute was punctuated by bouts of paranoia, violence and pyromania. What kind of life was that? What kind of family were they? What kind of mother had Faye been before her son's death? Surely it had been her infant son's death that had triggered all of this.

Otherwise, how could caring for the doll calm her so easily?

"You seem like a nice young man," Faye said, batting her thickly coated eyelashes at him.

He started, not expecting her to speak to him. He'd almost forgotten she was a person.

She sighed. "Miyuki is lovely isn't she?"

"Yes."

"She takes after her father's side. He was a wonderful man. I miss him very much." Tears flooded her eyes and he found himself leaning toward her in sympathy. "Ronin was the love of my life and I hate to say it because a mother shouldn't say these things about her children—" She covered the doll's ears. "—but she's my favorite. Always has been. I loved her father so much." She swiped at a tear. "I thought I'd die when he did. Do you know what that's like? Have you ever loved someone that much?"

He nodded. He loved her daughter that much.

"I can see you do. Good, because Miyuki needs that." She looked down at the bundle in her arms, then back at him. "I know it's a doll."

"You do?" His voice cracked under the pressure of an unnamable emotion.

She looked back down at the doll and started rocking and singing again.

"I'm ready," Mi said from behind him and he automatically reached for his gun, registering at the last moment that she wasn't a threat.

He popped out of his chair and took the bags from her.

"Let me grab the bassinet. Oh, and I'll need the car seat from my car," Mi said, her gaze on her mother.

"Give me your keys and I'll take care of it. You stay here." He looked back at Faye over his shoulder.

Mi opened a drawer in the kitchen and took out her spare key. "Here." She offered him the key, then shoved her hands in the back pockets of her jeans. "I'll go get the bassinet." She spun on her heel, leaving him holding a diaper bag and suitcase.

He didn't think twice about what he was doing. If he had, he'd likely have walked out the front door and kept right on walking. He was so far out of his depth, so far outside of ordinary that he'd need a new frame of reference for normal. He tried not to think about that as he unbuckled the car seat from Mi's car, buckled it into the backseat of his extended cab, and put the bassinet Mi gave him into the bed of his truck.

He watched as Mi took "Ethan" from her mother and strapped him into the car seat, then he helped them both into the truck and they were on their way. He'd noticed that Mi had tied a scarf around her neck in the middle of fucking summer. A scarf. To hide the bruises. He wanted to laugh. He wanted to cry. But most of all he wanted to punch the shit out of something.

They pulled up in front of an apartment building on the fringes of Dallas where families lived, kids played, and parents probably didn't try to choke their children to death. He escorted Mi and her mother carrying Ethan to the front door. Mi knocked. Then knocked again. Her brother answered the door after the third knock. He opened it with a scowl and the stale scent of whiskey on his breath.

They crossed the threshold, walking from suburbia to *Animal House* in a few short strides. Lucas had friends who had lived like this in their college days, but if he had to guess he would double down on Mi's brother not being a student. This level of lazy came from selfishness and a general I-don't-give-a-shit-about-anything attitude.

"Where's Mom supposed to sleep?" Mi asked her brother out of the side of her mouth. She eyed the pile of laundry on the couch.

"Sorry, I didn't have time to call the maid to have her spruce the place up before you came." Jason kicked an empty chip bag on his way to the couch.

Mi's brother picked up the laundry and threw it on the floor. From Lucas's angle, he couldn't tell if it was clean or dirty. He guessed it didn't really matter one way or the other to Jason since they were in the same shape as the clothes he wore.

Faye sat down on the couch, cradling her doll, and took up her rocking and singing again.

"Where can I put this?" Lucas asked, lifting the bassinet he carried.

Jason's gaze flew to Mi. "Are you shitting me?"

"Jas, please," Mi whispered. "It's just for a few days until I can figure a couple of things out."

"Fine. Whatever. But you owe me." Jason turned to Lucas. "Put that in the bedroom. I don't want anybody to see it."

Lucas found the bedroom in even worse shape. He put the crib-thing in a corner of the room, feeling almost guilty. Jason could live how he wanted, but his mother shouldn't have to step over her son's empty condom wrappers to get to the bathroom.

Fuck.

He walked back into the living area and straight into a harshly whispered argument between Mi and her brother.

"—two hundred then," Mi spat.

"Deal. But the price goes up if this goes longer than three days," Jason replied.

"What the hell is going on here?" Lucas asked.

"Nothing," Mi muttered, gluing her gaze on the floor.

Jason rocked back on his heels. "Just getting some things straight, man."

"Mi, why don't you show your mother where Ethan's things are so she knows?" Lucas said.

She gave him a quick, hard warning look, then took her mother into the bedroom.

Lucas turned to Jason and fished his wallet out of his back pocket. He drew out a five one hundred dollar bills and shoved them at Jason. "Take her to a decent fucking hotel for as long as it takes to find her another place to stay. This will get you started. Here's my card if you need more. And you don't take one dime from Mi. Got it?"

Jason bobbed his head, his eyes wide.

"You should wonder why your sister's wearing a scarf."

"What?"

"And keep your fucking mouth shut." He dropped another hundred into Jason's hand and put his wallet away.

Jason shoved the money in his front pocket. "Got it."

They turned as Mi reentered the room. Lucas had to hand it to Jason—the kid knew how to act, slipping back into his surly brother skin in the blink of an eye.

Mi's gaze bounced between the two men, then settled on Lucas's chin. "Can you please get the car seat out of your truck?"

"Sure." Lucas strolled to the truck, blindly trusting that Jason actually gave a shit about his sister.

By the time he got back with the car seat, Mi and her brother were going at it. Lucas hovered by the door just out of sight.

"Did that asshole do that to you?" Lucas heard Jason ask.

"No!"

"Then what the fuck, Mi? Who choked you?"

"Keep your voice down." There was a long silence and then Lucas heard Mi's voice, small and defeated. "Mom did it."

"*What*?"

"Ssh, be quiet."

Lucas picked that moment to walk back in. He took in Mi's stiff posture and Jason's fury flushed face. "What the hell's going on?" He should really take up acting.

Jason pointed at Mi's neck, directing his anger at Lucas. "Why did you bring our mom *here* instead of locking her up?"

In answer, Lucas turned to Mi.

Jason did the same. "Are you fucking kidding me, Mi? This has to stop. She's sick. She needs help. What the fuck were you thinking bringing her here?"

"Keep your voice down," Mi pleaded.

So the brother wasn't in on the big secret. Interesting, Lucas thought.

Jason's tone gentled. "Mi, she steals shit. She burns down houses. She takes care of a damn doll like a real baby. She fucking choked you. What else has to happen before you admit she needs help?"

Mi put a shaking hand to her forehead. "Back off, Jason."

"Mi," Jason urged. "She tried to kill you."

"I know!" Mi backed away, her whole body trembling. "Just do this please. I promise you it will be okay. She'll be okay. She's taking a nap right now." She looked up at her brother and what Lucas saw in her eyes nearly broke his heart.

He had to get her out of there. "We'll leave this discussion for now. I'm taking Mi home." He put an arm around her and herded her toward the door. "Let us know if anything... changes," he told Jason as they left.

On the way home Lucas tried to make sense of what had happened at Jason's apartment. The kid obviously cared about his sister. He and Lucas were on the same side as far as getting Faye help. And from the way it sounded, he'd been after Mi to do just that for some time now. So why wouldn't Mi get her mother help? Fuck it. As soon as he was alone he'd call Malcolm and get him to dig deeper into Faye's background and Ethan's death. He already had Malcolm chasing down Mi's missing friend Tracey, what was one more search?

They pulled into the parking garage of Lucas's building and into his parking spot. He cut the engine and sat back. Mi reclined against her seat, her head turned away. From this angle, he could see the marks on her neck, just turning to bruises. A strand of hair blocked a portion of it, but not enough to buffer the punch to the gut seeing her injured delivered.

He climbed out of the truck, came around to her side, and opened the door. She looked at him then, her eyes full of need. He unbuckled her seat belt and lifted her. She wrapped her arms around his neck loosely. He carried her through the lobby and up to the apartment. The lobby guards barely paid them any attention anymore. He went straight to the bathroom and sat her down on the toilet seat, then turned the faucets on the tub. When the water heated, he plugged the drain and adjusted the temperature.

Turning back around, he found her watching him.

"Thank you," she said.

"What for?"

She inched a shoulder up. "Everything. I know you don't want to hear it, but I really am sorry about everything that's happened. I bet you didn't count on all this when you took the job as my bodyguard."

"I didn't count on a lot of things." He walked over to her. "Arms up." He pulled her shirt over her head, then knelt down and took her shoes off. "I didn't count on you seeing more in me. I didn't count on how incredible the sex would be. Stand up." She did and he helped her out of her panties and jeans. "I didn't count on you having secrets." He paused. "That's not true. I knew from the way you looked at those pictures in Crosby's office when we first met that there was something you were hiding."

Sweeping her off her feet, he carried her to the bathtub and eased her in. "I didn't count on you surviving my family." He stripped in a matter of seconds, then stepped into the bath with her. "Mostly I didn't count on how hard and fast I'd fall for you." Leaning against the back of the tub, he closed his eyes and let the heat of the water seep into tired muscles.

"Lucas?"

"Hmm?"

She moved, sending the water swirling around him, and shut off the tap. "I... I want you to know..."

"Will you do me a favor, *querida*? No more talking for a while, okay?"

"Sure." More water eddied around him, lapping up his chest as she went back to her seat.

He tried to empty his mind and just be, but her foot brushed his leg, then her hand. The image of her breasts bobbing in the water every time she moved played behind his eyelids, making it hard to relax semi-erect. After a while, he gave in and let his mind wander up the dark alleys of every fantasy he'd ever had about her.

He was enjoying a rather good one where Mi was on her hands and knees in front of him dressed in... nothing. Then from out of nowhere she pulled out the pink blindfold and fuzzy handcuffs from her show. Huh. She clamped a cuff to the headboard, then to his wrist. All of a sudden she had another set and did the same to his other hand. She slipped the blindfold over his eyes and then she—

"Lucas?"

He nearly groaned in frustration. "No talking, remember?"

"Sorry. I was just wondering what your plans were for that massive hard on."

He cracked an eye open.

"I still owe you sixteen orgasms. I thought since you've already done most of the work for me..." Her smile finished the end of the sentence.

He started to return her smile, about to take her up on her offer, but then his gaze tracked up from her nipples, hard in the warm water, to her neck, reminding him of what she'd just been through. "Not now, *querida*. Maybe later."

She edged toward him, the water rippling with her movement, until she straddled his lap. "Come on." She wrapped her hand around his cock. "We could knock that number back to fifteen."

He grabbed her wrist, pulling her hand off him. "Not now."

She sat back. "Lucas—"

He saw the hurt in her eyes his rejection had caused and hated himself for putting it there. But he knew he'd hate himself more if he took what she was offering so soon after she'd been injured. Already his desire waned. He leaned forward and kissed her neck, circling the ring of bruises. She arched back and let him, her fingers laced in his hair.

He covered her neck with soft kisses, wishing for so many things: to make the marks disappear, to right the wrongs done to her, to take away her fear and pain, but most of all he wished she loved him. If she loved him she'd let him in. If she loved him she'd trust him. If she loved him he would never have to wish for anything ever again.

He folded her against his chest and held on, trying to imprint on his mind the feel of her skin against his, the slide of their wet flesh. She sighed and relaxed deeper against him. Fingering the ends of her hair, he was reminded of the first night she'd spent in his house. She'd sat on the floor next to him, the cat in her lap and he'd played with her hair just as he did now. He'd been fascinated by her, everything about her. And oh, God how he'd wanted her.

He wanted her still. That would never change. Buried deep inside her he found what he'd never expected… acceptance… a mate… a home…peace. He never wanted to be parted from her, couldn't imagine himself without her. That's why he'd backed off when she'd thrown down her ultimatum. He'd gone against instinct and let her have her way. He knew she'd been scared, backed into a corner. If he gave her time to think it through, he knew she'd see how not getting her mother help damaged them all. Especially herself.

He saw so much now, understood her better. Loved her more. But her threat still hung over them like a guillotine blade with her the one holding the rope. He wondered how long he could live like that, how long they could survive under it. Right now with her wrapped around him he felt like he could withstand anything.

"Lucas?"

"Hmm?"

"I'm okay, really."

"Maybe, but I'm not. Are you hungry? It's been hours since we grabbed those burgers."

"Sure." Mi climbed off him and watched him rise from the bath, the water sheeting down the hard planes of his body.

She'd tried to reach out to him, tried the method she knew best. There was a lot to make up for. Certainly more than a hand job could fix. She should tell him she loved him, but every time she'd opened her mouth something else had come out. So she'd gone back to the tried and true, the one thing between them that was easy and honest. And he'd rejected her.

She sat in the water long after he'd left the room, long after it had grown cold. Regret crept over her like a fog, obscuring all of her good intentions. She should never have gotten involved with Lucas and yet couldn't see how she could have stopped it. They'd brushed against each other like waves lapping the shore, leaving a piece of themselves and taking a little something from each other every time they'd touched, every time they'd made love. Until they'd taken too much and left behind more than they'd intended.

And now she didn't know where she ended and he began. He'd weathered the worst with her and was still here, battered, maybe a little broken, but still here. But for how long? How long until something else happened? She'd already gone too far, had drawn a line he couldn't cross. How long until he stopped trying to cross it and just walked away?

With a groan she rose out of the water and caught her reflection in the mirror over the vanity. She climbed out of the tub and walked dripping across the room for a better look. Oh, God. No wonder Lucas and Jason had freaked out. She leaned forward for a better look, hardly feeling the chill of the marble counter.

The awful look on her mother's face as her hands had pressed against Mi's neck came back full bore. Her eyes burning with hate, her teeth set hard to the task, the dots of spittle on her chin, her face compressed with the effort... that was not her mother, not the woman who had cared for and loved her. Where had that mother gone?

She eased back from the mirror.

"I ordered—" Lucas paused in the doorway, his gaze catching on hers in the mirror. "I got pizza," he finally finished.

"Okay."

He'd dressed in dark jeans and a black t-shirt, his feet bare. "It's a nice night. We could eat outside."

"I'd like that." She watched him leave, then sagged against the counter as soon as he'd gone.

She'd put the wall between them, she knew. But she couldn't take back the things she'd said or pretend she hadn't meant them. He hadn't asked any questions... yet. Soon he'd unload his questions and she'd stack them up with all of the others, building that wall higher until they wouldn't be able to see each other over the top.

CHAPTER 7

Mi fiddled with the edge of her napkin, folding and unfolding the corner. The awkwardness that had developed between her and Lucas was beginning to slide into arduous. They sat on the balcony, overlooking the Dallas skyline, the last dregs of pizza cold in front of them. They'd barely spoken except to pass this or hand over that. They were as polite as strangers, and that politeness ate away at her one please and one thank you at a time until she wanted to stand on the table and scream at the top of her lungs.

He hardly looked at her, his glances brushing over, then away. She missed his lingering looks, going from flicker to flame in an instant. Now it seemed as though looking at her was more than he could bear.

Her cell phone rang and her heart lodged in her throat. Pulling it out of her pocket, she dreaded what she'd see on the display, then let the breath she'd been holding out in a whoosh when she saw Lucy's number glowing on the screen.

"Hello?" she answered.

"Mi," Lucy panted. "I need you to come."

"What's wrong?" Out of the corner of her eye she saw Lucas sit up straighter.

"I'm in labor. Oh, Mi, I can't find Kevin anywhere. Ooohh," she moaned, then panted.

Mi waited, worrying for her friend.

"Mi?"

"I'm here. What do you mean you can't find him?"

"He's not answering his cell. I called everywhere. Please come. My mom's here and she's driving me crazy. She won't stop... ooohhh..."

"I'll be right there. Parkland Hospital, right?"

"Yeeessss."

"Hang on. I'm coming." Mi punched the phone off and ran back into the apartment with Lucas on her heels.

"What's going on?"

"Lucy's in labor. I have to get to the hospital. She needs me."

THEY WERE out the door in less than five minutes and standing outside Lucy's hospital room in less than twenty. Lucy's piercing scream came through the closed door, and Lucas's face lost all color.

"You should probably stay here," Mi told him.

He straightened his shoulders. "I go where you go."

"Uh-huh." She opened the door.

Lucy was lying in the bed, her feet in the stirrups. A nurse stood between her legs, her mother stood next to her bedside wringing her hands and reciting the Lord's Prayer.

"Mom, stop it!" Lucy barked, then let out a howl.

Lucas gave the room a quick scan and then stepped back, his face even whiter than before. "I'll... ah... wait here."

The door closed with Mi inside, the sound of her laughter echoing after her. Jesus. That was more than he ever wanted to see about the miracle of birth. If only he could wash his eyeballs. Leaning against the wall, he pulled out his phone, then spotted the no cell phone sign on the wall and shoved it back in his pocket.

A familiar voice caught his attention. He turned to see Cal leaning against the counter of the nurse's station. What was he doing here? Lucas strolled over and positioned himself so he could see Lucy's door.

"You're the last person I expected to see here," Lucas said to him.

"Hey, just taking care of something."

"In the maternity ward? Something you need to tell me, man?"

"What? No. Hell no. I'm here about Lucy."

Lucas raised his brows in reply.

"I guess you're here with Mi," Cal said, neatly changing the subject.

The nurse behind the counter slid a clipboard across to Cal. "If you'll just sign here, Mr. Sellers, we'll have that private room ready for Mrs. Walker when she delivers."

Cal signed the form and slid it back. "Thank you for your help," he told the nurse. "Anything she needs, you just send me the bill." Picking up his hat, Cal motioned for Lucas to follow him a short distance away.

"What's up?" Lucas asked.

"I'm glad Mi's here. Lucy's going to need her."

"What do you mean?"

"Don't say anything to Mi about this yet. I don't want this moment ruined for Lucy." Cal lowered his voice even more. "Her husband isn't going to be here to see his child born." There was a bitterness to Cal's words that made Lucas wonder if there had ever been anything personal between Cal and Lucy. "He's been arrested."

"Damn. What for?"

"Polygamy."

"Are you shitting me?"

Cal's lips flattened. "Wish I was."

"How do you know about this and Lucy doesn't?"

"I have my ways."

Which meant Cal had something to do with Lucy's husband's arrest either directly or indirectly. Yeah, definitely something personal going on there.

Cal slid his hat on. "And as far as Lucy knows, I was never here."

"You don't want credit for the private room?"

"Like I said, I don't want this moment ruined for Lucy. My being within a hundred feet of her—hell my being in the same city—would do it." Cal started to back away. "I was never here." He gave Lucas a two-fingered salute and sauntered off.

MI WASN'T sure if she was holding Lucy's hand or not. Her hand had gone numb sometime between Lucy's second and fifth push as best as she could remember. Everything was happening faster now. The doctor was there. Lucy's son of a bitch husband wasn't. Mi would never forgive him for leaving Lucy to give birth to their child alone. She'd left at least eight voicemail messages while Lucy screamed in the background.

"One, two, three... *push!*" the nurse coached.

"That's it, Lucy. Good girl. I see the head. We're almost there," the doctor said.

"And rest." The nurse replaced the oxygen mask over Lucy's nose and mouth as Lucy flopped back onto the bed.

Mi smoothed Lucy's hair back. "You're doing so good. Brie will be here before you know it."

Lucy pulled the mask up. "Fuck him. I'm naming her Poppy like I wanted to."

"That's right. You're doing all the work," Mi soothed. "Name her whatever you want."

"Again!" the nurse barked.

A few moments later Poppy came into the world screaming her lungs out. Mi swore she'd never seen a more perfect baby.

"She has red hair." Lucy's voice was full of wonder. "My grandma had red hair."

"Strawberry blond," Mi agreed. "And blue eyes. She's so beautiful, Lucy."

"Thank you for being with me." Lucy's eyes filled with tears. "I couldn't have done it without you. I can't believe

Kevin wasn't here." She bent forward and kissed her daughter's hand. "Oh, Mi. Where could he be?"

"I don't know. I'm so sorry."

"I want you to pick her middle name."

"Oh, no. I couldn't."

"Yes. You can." Lucy dragged her arm across her eyes, wiping away her tears. "I want you to."

"Okay." Mi looked down at the baby and her mind went blank. All at once it hit her that this would be the only opportunity she'd ever have to name a child. She smoothed a hand over the soft down of the baby's hair, totally awestruck by the enormity of her task. She was going to chose a name that would stay with this child forever. "Victoria."

"Poppy Victoria Walker," Lucy said, looking down at her sleeping daughter. "I like it." She beamed up at Mi. "It's fits her, don't you think?"

"Perfectly."

Mi sat with her friend until Lucy's eyes grew heavy with sleep. She left her with a promise to visit the next day and walked out into the hall where she found Lucas waiting for her. He rose from the chair he'd procured from somewhere and met her in the middle of the hallway.

"Everything all right?" he asked.

"Yeah, she's so small and perfect. Lucy was a champion. I don't know how she did it without drugs."

"With a lot of screaming and yelling from what I could hear."

She chuckled and leaned into him. "That's for sure."

"Let's go. It's nearly dawn." He put an arm around her and steered them to the elevator bank.

She suppressed a huge yawn that slid right back into the goofy smile she'd worn ever since little Poppy Victoria came into the world. "Lucy asked me to chose her middle name."

"Yeah?"

The elevator doors opened and they stepped into the car. Lucas punched the button and the doors slid closed.

"I chose Victoria after my mother's mother." She sighed and leaned into him. "I can't believe Kevin missed his daughter's birth. I could kill him. He doesn't deserve either one of them."

The doors opened and they walked out of the elevator.

"Some people don't realize what they've got until it's gone," he said.

Something about his words struck her. A hidden message meant for her perhaps? Was he issuing a warning? She looked up at him, but he gazed ahead, navigating them through the unusually crowded main entrance.

As they made their way to the exit, a large crowd came through the doors at once, pushing them back to one side. Someone knocked into her shoulder, sending her backward and out of Lucas's embrace. He reached for her and then he was hit from the side, spinning him the other direction. Standing on tiptoes, she could see his head above the others and tried to move in that direction.

Something stroked her palm and then a fist closed

around her hand. She turned to see who had touched her and was brushed back by a couple rushing through the doors. A man rushed past, shoving her shoulder and turning her into a woman who complained. She could no longer see Lucas. Panic swamped her. She swung her head one direction then the other, looking for him. Nothing.

A hand clamped down on her arm and she spun around to strike out. Lucas pulled her into his chest. She grabbed ahold of him with both hands, relieved to have finally found him. He steered them to an out of the way corner and wrapped his arms around her.

"Are you all right?" he asked, examining her.

She put a hand over her heart, which still beat out a ragged rhythm. She hadn't noticed. In all the confusion, she didn't realize that the stranger had pressed something into her palm. She held out her hand up and unfolded her fingers. A small square of white paper that had been folded over and over until it was about one inch by one inch lay in her palm.

"What is it?" Lucas asked.

She turned, trying to spot the person who could have put it there. Lucas grabbed her shoulder, bringing her back around to him.

"What's the matter?"

"Somebody put this in my hand."

He looked down at her palm, then around, his hand going for his gun. "Who? Where?" Grabbing her arm, he pulled her behind him. "Who was it? Where'd they go?"

"I don't know. I got jostled and then somebody brushed my hand, pressing this paper into it. I never saw them."

He backed her into a corner, all the while keeping her between him and the crowd. "Are you sure? Did they say anything to you?"

"No, nothing. Just this in my hand. I should open it."

"No. Leave it for Rolls."

She thought about arguing, but she knew he was right. "What are all these people doing here at this hour?"

"I heard one of the nurses in maternity talking about a huge pile up on thirty-five. Buses or something." He scanned the thinning crowd. "Let's get out of here. I don't like this."

Reaching back, he took her hand and pulled her until she was tucked along his side. He rushed her to the truck and had it in gear, backing out of the parking space before she could clamp her seatbelt on. He took side streets, changing lanes, and turning until she wasn't even sure they were pointed in the right direction. She didn't take a real gulp of air until the gate of his parking garage rolled down after them.

Back in his apartment, Mi dropped the paper onto the coffee table and stared down at it as though it would rise up and eat her whole.

Lucas sat down next to her. "All right. Go over it again. Tell me everything you remember, any impressions or feelings you got. Anything."

She closed her eyes and pictured it, then cursed herself for being so fixed on Lucas's words about not appreciating someone until they were gone. If she'd paid better attention, she might have noticed more. She retold the story, pressuring her brain for more details until she'd worked herself into a headache.

"That's all." She finally gave up, feeling as though she'd let Lucas down in a whole new way.

"It's late. You might remember more after some rest."

"Hmm, maybe." She pointed to the square of paper. "What do we do with that?"

"I'll bag it up for Rolls and leave him a voice mail to call us—" He checked his watch. "—in about five or six hours. Why don't you go get ready for bed?"

"Yeah." She made a move to go, but he grabbed her hand and pulled her back.

"Hey, you did good. Don't beat yourself up. You had a really long night with Lucy. I'm sure the hospital has cameras that Rolls can access. With any luck he'll get an image he can work with."

"Yeah, okay."

He released her and she trudged down the hall to the bathroom to get ready for bed. As she entered the bedroom, the first rays of sunrise crested the horizon, beaming light of the new day into the room. She stood at the window for a moment, basking in the wonder of the dawn. New beginnings were supposed to bring hope and clarity, a chance to start over with the lessons learned from the day before.

If yesterday had taught her anything, it was that nothing stayed the same. Old aches could become new hurts, new hurts faded to aches. Joy could turn to sorrow, sorrow to joy. And that nothing was ever given that couldn't be taken away.

She turned away from the window, feeling older than she should. The image of Lucy with her new daughter brought a smile to her face and just like that the world on her shoulders lifted a little.

Lucas bagged up the square of paper and left a message for Rolls as he said he would. Thank God Gann hadn't tried to do more than deliver a message. Lucas didn't even care what it said. He just wanted the bastard caught. He jotted off a quick text to Cal to let him know that Lucy and the baby were okay. Cal hadn't asked him to, but if it had been Mi he wouldn't have slept until he knew all was well.

He lay down on the couch. He did his best thinking lying down. Now that he finally had a thinking couch, his thoughts dried up. Staring at the ceiling as the sun came up, he felt like a colossal failure. The bastard had gotten to Mi again. And with him only feet away. Fuck. The look on her face as she opened her hand and showed him the paper.

Gooch jumped up on the couch and curled on top of his stomach. He didn't have the energy to knock the cat off. Bits of thoughts sparked, but none took light. He couldn't even chase one down to complete it. God, he was tired. He let his eyes drift closed, but sleep was a fickle bitch and didn't see fit to visit him.

He wondered if Mi slept and if she did, did she dream? Did he make the cut? Did she ever imagine a future for them? Or did she keep him firmly in the here and now? He wondered why he tortured himself. What was it about that woman that turned him inside out and upside down until he wasn't sure who or what he was to her? His gut churned, burning from the crappy hospital coffee the nurses had given him out of pity.

He tried to get a read on Mi, but every time he thought he had her nailed, she pulled up his stakes and threw them in his face. God, he was a masochist. Or a fucking idiot. It was hard to tell which. And then he'd look into her amber eyes and his world would tilt, bringing his bubble back into plumb. Oh, she was the one for him all right. Now he just had to figure out a way to convince her of that.

The last thought he had before sleep finally came for him was of her, her belly rounded and full with his child.

Yup, he was a fucking idiot for sure.

CHAPTER 8

Mi woke up alone in the big bed. The light of mid-day beamed through the wall of screened windows onto the bed. The bottom of her stomach plummeted when she realized she'd slept the whole night alone. Scrambling out of bed, she tossed the covers aside and ran out into the living room. Empty. She looked in the kitchen. Also empty. The sick feeling in her stomach swelled until she had to put a hand out. She caught herself on the doorframe to the kitchen and tried to tamp down the rising panic.

And then she heard the soft buzz saw of his snore and sagged against the doorframe in relief. She found him lying on his back on the couch, one arm thrown over his eyes, the other hanging off the side of the couch nearly to the floor. He was still dressed in his clothes from the night before. The cat looked up at her from his place on Lucas's stomach and meowed. She plucked Gooch up and cradled him under her chin. Why hadn't Lucas come to bed?

He'd hardly touched her since pulling her mother off of her the day before. And now he'd slept on the couch instead of sharing the bed with her. She should be relieved he was pulling away from her. Their break would be so much easier if they both wanted it. And yet she couldn't summon up any gladness. All that came was the pounding sadness that she would once again be alone. She could stand loneliness and had for too long, but now she'd have to endure it with the knowledge of what it was like to love and be loved by Lucas.

She reached out and fingered the lock of hair slanting across his forehead. He stirred and then his dark gaze fastened on hers, the intensity of his stare going through her like a bolt of lightening. Then his attention caught on the marks on her neck and a frown dug deep between his brows. Pulling her hand back, disappointment spread through her like a toothache. He didn't see her the same anymore. The bruises her mother's fingers had left behind were a brutal reminder of all the ways she had and would let him down.

His cell phone rang. So easily he turned away from her to answer it.

He dug it out of his pocket. "Hello? Yeah. Half an hour. See you then." He hung up the phone and stood. "Rolls is on his way over."

"I guess I'd better get dressed," she replied.

Rolls arrived with a ketchup stain on his tie and a cloud of sad resignation floating around him. He dropped into a recovered, over-stuffed chair Mi had picked up off the curb. "I've got some news," he began. "We arrested your friend Tracey Casey for the studio bombin' and murder of Davy Johnson. I'm sorry," he added, with a nod for Mi.

"No. I don't believe it," Mi said.

Lucas reached over and grabbed Mi's hand. "You have proof she did it?" he asked Rolls.

"Had enough to bring her in for questionin'. She's confessed. Gave up everythin' on that religious organization C.A.L.M. and their leader Cookie Dixon. I'm surprised ya'll haven't heard. Been all over the news. That senator and congresswoman who backed 'em have been on every channel that would show their faces, tryin' to talk their way out of it."

"Confessed?" Mi leaned into Lucas's shoulder, the heavy weight of disappointment and sorrow pressing down on her like a vice. She couldn't believe it. Tracey had killed Davy. Had tried to kill *her*.

"Your friend Davy's funeral's tomorrow. One o'clock at the Pentecostal church on Bickers. You said you'd want to know," Rolls said.

"Thank you," Mi managed to whisper.

Rolls nodded in acceptance, his jowls collapsing like bellows. "Ya said you had somethin' to show me?"

Lucas handed Rolls the plastic bag with the square of paper inside. "Mi was... given this at the hospital early this morning."

Rolls examined the paper inside the bag, turning it back and forth in front of the window. "Can't see nothin'." Dropping his hand holding the bag between his legs, he looked at Mi. "Tell me what happened."

Mi recited her story, pressing her brain for every detail. She suddenly remembered something she'd left out before. "Peppermint. I remember getting a whiff of peppermint. Really strong."

Rolls jotted that down in his notebook along with the other notes he'd made. "Anythin' else?"

"No. That's it. Sorry."

"Do you want to know what the paper says?" Rolls asked.

Mi shook her head, then changed her mind. "Actually, yes. I would."

Rolls pulled a pair of latex gloves from his suit pocket and drew the note out of the plastic bag. Lucas squeezed Mi's hand as Rolls unfolded the small paper.

His brows wadded up over his nose. "I'm coming for you. Be ready," he read.

"Jesus fuck," Lucas said.

Rolls put the note back in the bag. "Sorry."

"Just please catch him so I can go back to my life, my home. I'm tired of being scared all the time."

"I'm doing my best for you." They rose as Rolls did and followed him to the elevator doors. He turned back. "I'm sorry 'bout your friend. I'll keep you updated as things go along. And if I hear anythin' on Gann, I'll letchya know."

"Thank you, detective," Lucas said, shaking his hand.

"Yes, thank you." Pressing her teeth into her bottom lip, Mi wrapped her arms around herself and headed down the hall to the bedroom. She leaned against the window. The city gleamed below, people going about their day as though nothing bad would ever happen to them. She'd been one of those people.

How could she have been so *wrong* about Tracey? They'd worked so closely together, saw each other every-day. They went out for drinks, dinner, caught a movie now and then. How could Tracey have done this? Had she been planning this all along? Had Tracey faked their friendship to advance C.A.L.M.'s agenda? Had Tracey only been friendly just so she could get close enough to kill? God.

Gann was coming for her, expecting her to be ready for him. Why was he doing this? What had she done to attract his attention? The trembling started as a shiver. Before she knew it she was shaking hard enough to make her teeth clack together.

"*Querida.*" Lucas came from behind her and wrapped his arms around her, bringing her into his warmth. "Ssh, I'm here."

She didn't want him to know how much Gann's note shook her so she went for the second equally awful thing. "Tracey was my friend. How could I have been so wrong about her?"

"Come and sit down with me." He brought her over to the couch at the foot of the bed. "I know it's hard when someone you care about deceives you."

Mi thought about his ex-fiancée and how Vanessa had deceived him in the worst way. "I guess you would know about that."

He gave a brief nod of acknowledgement.

"I lost two friends in that bombing," she said, looking out at the Dallas skyline. "Davy and Tracey." She wished she could cry, maybe that would release the aching knot that had a strangle-hold on her chest. "I don't have very many friends."

"You have me."

"Do I?" She couldn't keep the dull edge of doubt from turning her words hard.

"If you want me."

She looked at him then, weighing his sincerity. What she saw tugged at the knot in her chest, loosening it a little. "Lucas, I..." What? What would she do? Promise him the forever she saw in his eyes, knowing she couldn't follow through? No, she wouldn't do that to him. "Why did you sleep on the couch last night?" The question slipped out without having shaped into thought.

"I didn't mean to, but that couch is really comfortable," he said with a hint of nervous laughter. "I might just keep it."

"We could work something out. Like a time share or something."

"That wouldn't work for me. I'm an all or nothing kind of guy."

She couldn't answer, the words crashing against the back of her throat like an eighteen-car pile up. They were right there fully formed yet immobile, all the things she wanted to say.

Disappointment flashed briefly across his face before he set her hand in her lap and stood up. "Are you hungry?" he asked lightly.

As if cued, her stomach rumbled.

"I'll take that as a yes," he said, one corner of his mouth kicking up. "Do you want to go out or stay in?"

"Stay in."

They ordered some food and ate it in front of the TV, watching an action adventure movie Lucas chose. Mi picked up the remains of her dinner, purposely missing the bloody fight at the end of the movie. She took the opportunity to call Jason in the privacy of the kitchen.

"Hey, I was just calling to check in. How's Mom?"

"Hang on a sec." She could hear the TV in the background and then quiet. "She's okay," he said after a few moments. "Hasn't tried to choke me or anything so I guess that's good."

Mi ignored his dig. "But she seems calm?"

"Yeah, maybe even a little calmer than usual. How's your throat?"

"It's okay." She fingered the scarf around her neck, not wanting to tell him about the scratches and bruises that had bloomed to a violent bluish purple.

"You know I only went along with what you wanted because of the studio bombing. But I'm telling you, Mi, this is it. She pulls one more crazy ass stunt and I'm turning her in. Whether you okay it or not."

"Jason, no. Please promise me you won't do that."

"I'm not making that promise."

"Please, Jas."

"She tried to *kill* you."

Mi could feel the panic swelling up in her chest. "Jason, if you do that I will take her and move and you will never see us again. I mean it."

"Mi—"

"I mean it."

"What the hell's going on in here?" Lucas asked from the kitchen doorway.

"Damn it, Mi," Jason growled.

"I gotta go. Don't forget what I said." Mi clicked the phone off before he could respond.

Lucas leaned against the doorframe, arms crossed over his chest. "I take it that was Jason."

She didn't respond, thinking about how she could go around him and avoid the coming conversation all together.

"You'd rather move, leaving your brother, your job, your life than get your mother the help she needs?"

"That's none of your business."

"None of my business. Haven't we been over this?"

"I don't want to talk about this right now." She made a move to go around him, but he blocked her, filling the doorway.

"What are you hiding?"

"Nothing." But she couldn't meet his gaze, couldn't give him the answers he wanted.

"Oh, you're hiding something all right and I'm going to find out what it is. Either you can tell me yourself or Malcolm will find out what it is for me."

Her gaze snapped up to his. "You're having me *investigated*?"

"What has you so scared you're willing to throw away your life to protect it?"

"Leave it alone." She shoved at him, her efforts as useless as pushing on a brick wall. "Let me go."

"No. Not until you tell me what's going on. What affects you affects me."

Her laugh sounded sharp and harsh, an echoing alarm that she was on the edge of her control. "None of this affects you. Don't you get it? We're temporary. As soon as Doyle Gann is caught whatever this is between us is over."

"Is that what you want?"

"That's what is." She made a back and forth motion between them. "This was never going to last. We let off some steam, that's all. It was great. Really great. But it was just sex." Her argument sounded hollow even to her ears.

He gave her a pitying look. "Just some really great sex. Sure." He pivoted, giving her room to pass. "Good night. I hope you sleep well... fuck buddy," he said just as she went by him.

She kept walking, the stabbing pain of his words making it difficult to breathe. She'd asked for it, provoked him, but that didn't make it hurt less. Didn't make what she was doing any easier. It was the right thing, making the break early. It would be better in the long run, she repeated to herself a dozen or more times as she lay alone in the big bed that night with Lucas back in the spare bedroom down the hall.

The scent of their nights together on the sheets brought images of their bodies twisted and twined. She hugged his pillow, the smell of him mocking her every time she inhaled. The cat leapt on the bed and curled into the small of her back. At least she wouldn't be alone with her memories.

Lucas awoke to darkness and silence. But something was off. He could feel it in the air. He listened hard, straining to separate out the normal household noises from what had woken him up. Nothing. The sense of wrongness came again, this time stronger. Yeah, definitely off. He put his hand on his gun, lifting it from the nightstand without a sound. Using the skills he'd honed over the years, he climbed out of bed, controlling his movements and breathing.

He crept down the hall. His only thought was to get to Mi and make sure she was safe. Hugging the wall, gun in hand at his side, he moved closer to the master bedroom. A low murmur then a gasp from the bedroom brought his head up. Everything in him screamed for him to rush the room. His training kicked in, quickly tamping down that instinct. More deep whispers, then a squeak of protest suddenly cut off. He adjusted his grip on the gun as the outline of a man against the light of the windows came into view.

In the dimness he could make out Mi on the bed looking up at the man, her head back, her hair fisted in his hand. Fury, white-hot and rabid, exploded through him. He raised his gun and waited, sighting a kill shot. He had to be sure the bastard didn't have a weapon on her. The man pulled her from the bed. Her muffled yelp arrowed through him. She resisted the intruder's efforts to drag her toward the door, toward Lucas. Good girl.

Lucas inched closer. He ran a hand along the wall inside the bedroom. The man hauled her up, speaking in a harsh murmur. Mi nodded, her head bobbing up and down in instant agreement. With a smothered sob, she stopped resisting. The fucking bastard reached down and cupped her ass, bringing her up against his body. He whispered something, then chuckled, grinding his pelvis into her stomach. Fuck.

Lucas flipped the light switch, bathing the room in light. The first thing he noted was the knife in Gann's hand pressed against Mi's throat.

His finger tensed on the trigger. "Let her go."

Pulling Mi around in front of him, Gann laughed. "I'm taking what I came for." He jerked her head back by her hair, rubbing the edge of the blade along the bruises on her neck. He licked her cheek. "You and me got a date to keep. Ain't that right, sweet thing?"

Mi leaned back against Gann, gripping his knife arm, barely keeping her balance on tiptoe. Her eyes wide, mouth parted, she stared at Lucas, scarcely breathing. One false move and she'd come down on the knife at her throat. Lucas had the shot to the head. But Mi would go down when Gann did. Lucas kept his focus on Gann's movement.

"How'd you get in here?" Lucas asked, watching for an opening, waiting for a shot that wouldn't risk Mi.

"Well, see, that's an interesting story. But I don't have time for that now."

"Probably be all lies anyway," Lucas taunted.

Gann tightened his hold on Mi, the blade slid against her skin. A thin trickle ran down her neck from where he'd pierced her. The blood pounded in Lucas's ears, his vision narrowed, hazed over in red.

"The bitches love me, always have. You'll see, baby," Gann said to Mi. "I fuck real good. Your neighbor thought so," he said to Lucas. "Paid her a little attention and she practically fell on her back, legs spread. See, I been watching. Watching and waiting. Picked the right bird and she brings me right in."

Gann glanced around. "Her apartment's not as nice as this, but that didn't matter for what I had in mind. Knew what floor you were on, figured I'd kill two birds with one stone." He chuckled to himself. "Two birds. One stone. Get it?" The knife glinted.

"Still doesn't explain how you got in," Lucas said, sliding into the room.

"This building's just like pussy, once you're in, you're golden. It's the getting in that's the trick and I got in." He winked at Mi. "Then I got in. And here I am, baby, just like I promised."

"Let her go and I'll let you live," Lucas replied.

Gann snorted. "You don't get it. She don't come with me and I won't care if I live or die."

"And you don't get that she's not going anywhere with you."

"I'll kill her. And welcome death. We can't be together in life." Gann jerked Mi's head. "We'll be together in death."

The coldness of Gann's words seemed to freeze something in Mi. She looked at Lucas as though she *wanted* to give up. "I'll go," Mi conceded, drawing Gann's arm down. "Let us pass, Lucas."

Gann's face split into a terrible smile of triumph. "You heard her. Move back, asshole!"

Lucas could see that Mi had her feet under her now. He took a half step to the side, away from the door, his gun still trained on the center of Gann's forehead. They shifted toward him.

"Go on. Get back," Gann ordered, caressing the side of Mi's face with the hand that had held her hair. "My baby and me's got plans. I've waited three years. I came for you just like I said I would, didn't I, baby?"

Lucas took another step, keeping at an angle.

"Yes, you did," Mi replied, her gaze fastened on Lucas. "Just like you promised."

"I'm good at keeping promises. I'm gonna do all those things I wrote you about in my letter." Gann ran his hand down her chest, pinching at her breast.

Mi's eyes widened, her lips pressing together. Rage burned a scorching path through Lucas, wavering his vision.

"Uh, you like that, do you?" Gann asked her, pressing into her from behind. "Feel that? That's all for you, baby. Just wait till I get you alone."

Mi seemed to sigh in enjoyment, sagging a little, drawing Gann off balance. Lucas took the shot. Just as he'd trained. Gann's expression flipped from cocky to shocked. He spiraled backwards in a slow motion arc.

Mi used her grip on Gann's arm to push herself away from Gann and the knife. Lucas rushed her, catching her before she hit her head on the side of the bed. He kicked the knife away even though it was clear the fucker was dead.

Lucas cradled her against him. "Jesus, *querida*. Are you all right?"

She tilted her head back. "I think he might have

nicked me, but I'm okay." She shuddered. "He had his hands on me... the things he said..."

He examined her neck, frowning over the shallow cuts oozing blood. "He can't ever get to you again."

"He's... dead?"

Lucas would make the shot again, would have made it even sooner had it been safe, but that assertion did little to relieve the grimness of taking a life. "Yeah."

She looked up at him, her amazing amber eyes shining with unshed tears. He swallowed hard. How did she see him now? He'd done what he had to. Given the choice he'd do it again. Would that change how she viewed him?

"Thank you," she whispered.

Aw, fuck. Gratitude. "Don't."

She reached up and stroked the side of his face. "I know it wasn't easy for you."

"Easier than seeing him paw at you."

"I'm glad he's dead."

He glanced down at the still form, slowly bleeding into his bedroom carpet. He felt something close to gladness—relief, maybe? "Let's get you out of here. We need to call Rolls and report this."

AN HOUR AND A HALF LATER, the apartment swarmed with cops and a tech crew. Lucas sat in the living room with Rolls. Mi was with another detective in the kitchen. They'd confiscated Lucas's gun, which he expected. Rolls took Lucas through his story again, asking a lot of the same questions he had the first time around.

"We'll talk again," Rolls finally said. "I'm not gonna arrest you tonight. Chances are there won't be any charges, but you're gonna need to stay in town."

"Sure. We'll probably stay at a hotel tonight. You've got my cell number."

Rolls stood as Mi came into the room with the other detective and addressed his comments to her. "From what we can tell, looks like Gann acted alone."

"So it's over," she said, relief making her words a sigh.

"Yeah," Rolls answered, his gaze flicking back and forth between Lucas and Mi. "Looks like. You're free to go. Smith'll go with you to pack a bag if you want."

Mi nodded and followed the other detective into the bedroom.

An officer approached Rolls and whispered something to him. "Jesus H. Christmas! Are you sure?" The officer answered too low for Lucas to hear. "Shoot." Rolls responded. "All right. Better have the tech guys head on down there next. I'll be along shortly." Rolls shook his head, turning back to Lucas. "We found that neighbor Gann talked 'bout," Rolls said to Lucas. "Dead."

"Damn."

"You saved the tax payers a lot of money." Rolls nudged Lucas with his elbow, that just-us-buds smile accordioning his face. "Nice placement. Right to the center of the forehead." He shook his head. "Sure you don't want to come over to our side? We could sure use you, what with your training and all."

There was nothing except a black hole in Lucas

where the expected pride should have been. What was there to be proud of? He wasn't sorry Gann was dead, but he wasn't happy about it either. "I'll think about it." He wouldn't. He admired cops, he just didn't see himself as ever being one.

Rolls reached up and clapped him on the shoulder. "You do that. You do that. I'd best check on things in the other room. You take care of your lady." He left Lucas standing in the living room with people moving around him like a rock in a stream.

Lucas didn't correct him. Mi wasn't his lady or anything else at the moment. His role as her bodyguard was officially over. He jammed his hands in the front pockets of his jeans. She'd made it clear their time was limited. Hell, she'd pretty much said it was already over. So where did that leave them now?

Mi came back into the room, carrying two overnight bags and a pet carrier. "I crated Gooch and packed some things for you, too." She handed him one of the bags.

He took that one and the other one as well. "Are you ready?"

"Sure."

Wanting to remember how things once were, he gave the apartment one last look with all of Mi's things in it. They'd all go back tomorrow, along with her, most likely. Dawn crested, tinting the buildings orange and yellow and casting that light into the room in thin golden rays. Over. Finished. Complete. How sick was he that he almost wished Gann wasn't dead? Wished they had more time to work things out.

They stepped into the elevator and stood side by side, staring up at the decreasing numbers in silence.

MI CAST LUCAS AN UNCERTAIN GLANCE. He'd been so quiet since the shooting. She worried about him. Knowing his past, she understood how hard it had been for him to pull the trigger. He'd given up that life when he'd left the military and yet here he was back in it to defend her. She slipped her hand into his. Out of the corner of her eye she caught his surprise at the gesture.

She gave his hand a little squeeze. "Where are we going?"

"I was thinking a hotel."

The unspoken question was there, dangling in the spaces between his words. He was giving her the choice. In or out? With me or not? She drifted closer, leaning against his arm. She was grateful for what he'd done for her, but it wasn't gratitude that colored her decision. She wanted one more night with him, one night to show him all of the things she couldn't say. One more chance to give back a fraction of what he'd given her. One more night in his arms, in his bed. One more memory to take and one to leave.

"I'd like that," she replied, meeting his gaze in their reflection in the doors. "I'd like that a lot."

CHAPTER 9

The hotel room door closed behind Lucas with a quiet snick. They stood a few feet apart, a few feet from the yawning king sized bed. The air between them hummed, coming to life with all that lay between them. They drifted toward one another. There was no signal or glance, no plan or thought, just raw need drawing them together like opposite poles of a magnet.

He touched the side of her face with his fingertips. Their gazes locked in a battle of what if's and should we's. In the end, Mi supposed it didn't matter. If they were in the same room they'd want each other. It was more of a *when* than an *if*.

"It will always be like this, you know," he said this with certainty.

He wasn't telling her anything she didn't know. They'd waged a battle with no war. They'd conquered yet hadn't won. They'd survived the world, but not each other.

She reached for his wrist, laying her cheek against his palm. "I know."

He looked so lost. She was, too. He took her face in his hands and kissed her, a long, spiraling kiss that unwound the knots. His lips fit over hers, their tongues dancing a rhythm that beat back any residual doubt. He jerked at her clothing, a sign of his impatience. Smoothing her hands under his shirt, she drew it over his head. Her shirt hit the floor next to his. They wrestled with their remaining clothes, a flurry of movement punctuated with searing kisses and desperate touches. Their frantic hunger for each other mirrored their first time as though all their other times together hadn't assuaged their desire.

They hit the bed in a twist of limbs and roving hands. His mouth was everywhere, one breast then the other, her neck, her mouth and back again. She kissed a trail up his chest to the spot just under his jaw that drove him insane. He groaned, his hands sliding to her backside where he held her to him, his erection pressing insistently against her. She reached for him, wrapping her fingers around his long, hard length.

Keeping his mouth on hers, he reached for his pants, fumbling through the pockets. He pressed the foil packet into her hand, then slid his fingers between her legs, stroking her to desperation. She fit the condom on with more speed than finesse. He growled, turning them so she was on top. She held him to her, then slowly sank down. Their gazes met, held. What she saw in the dark depth of his eyes both thrilled and frightened her.

She set the pace, rising, then sinking down with slow deliberation, watching his eyes darken into black pools of pleasure. He grasped her hips, holding on, but not hurrying her. She bent and flicked her tongue over his nipple. God, that noise he made. She did it again to the other side, eliciting the same half moan, half growl. She loved pleasuring him, loved making him crazy with need.

She came down harder, faster, her own need a growing, gnawing thing. He met her thrusts, his hips flexing up in time with hers. She planted her hands on his chest, using the leverage to increase the pace. He writhed beneath her, holding her tighter. So close... He reached between them, his thumb sliding through her slickness. There... just there. She arched back, her fingers pressing into his chest and came with his name on her lips. Driving into her one more time, he came with roar, grinding deeper into her.

She flopped down onto his chest, her hair trailing out around her. Still vibrating from her orgasm, she closed her eyes, shuddering in the aftermath. Her breath puffed across his chest, her heart banging against her ribcage. He was right. It would always be like this between them. It was like he was made for her, knew just how to please her. She understood him, wanted him, loved him. There would never be another man in her life like him.

"I love you," she whispered into his chest.

If he heard her, he gave no sign. The stroke of his hand up and down her back never stalled or wavered. She breathed a sigh of relief.

"I love you too, *querida*," he said, almost too quiet to hear if it weren't for her ear pressed to his chest.

She closed her eyes, replaying his words over again in her head, savoring the shape of them and the way her heart sped up. For a few moments she imagined a life where they could say these words to each other everyday in passing as she'd seen other couples do. Throwing the phrase like invisible confetti to flutter and float about, blanketing the ground around them. Didn't those other people know how lucky they were?

She scrambled off him, mumbling that she needed the bathroom.

"Oh, shit."

Something about the way he'd said that had her halting in her tracks. She turned.

He was sitting up in bed looking down at himself, then up at her. His lips parted, his eyes wide with shock, he dropped a bomb that nearly took her to her knees.

"The condom broke."

Her hand flew to her mouth. No. This couldn't be happening. She fumbled for the doorknob, needing it for balance. "Tell me you're joking."

He shook his head back and forth.

"How could you let this happen?" she wailed. "Oh my God." She sank down slowly to the floor, her back pressed against the wall. "Oh my God. Oh my God." She couldn't have a baby. Just the thought of it... oh, God no. She just couldn't.

He got up, removed the offending condom, wrapped it in a tissue and threw it away. Crouching down next to her, he stroked her hair. "It'll be all right."

She batted his hand away. "How can you say that? I'm not on the pill. Don't you get it?" She shoved away from him. What was wrong with him? "We have to do something."

He stood and watched her pace. Just stood there like it was no big deal.

"Don't just stand there, do something!" she shouted at him.

"Calm down. It was just one time."

"That's all it takes!" The bubbling broth of her emotions bumped the lid she'd so carefully kept over them, threatening to knock it off completely. "I can't have this baby."

He sat down on the edge of the bed, calm as ever. "If you're pregnant we'll deal with it."

She stopped her pacing and stared at him. He wasn't serious, they never were. All their promises vanished right about the time the possibility of pregnancy became the reality of a baby. She'd seen her mother go through it with Jason's father and then Ethan's.

"I'll get that morning after pill."

He launched off the bed toward her. "Wait. Let's talk about this."

"I'm not having this baby."

"There might not be a baby, but if there is we'll work it out." He actually looked like he might be happy about the possibility.

She snorted in disbelief. "You say that now, but you don't mean it." Derision turned her words nasty and accusing.

"Don't tell me what I mean and don't mean." He swelled to his full size, more angry than she'd ever seen him.

"You don't get it." She ticked points off on her fingers. "You won't be the one raising it by yourself. You won't be the one taking care of it day and night. You won't be the one working all day just to come home to more work."

He edged closer. "You wouldn't be alone."

"That's what they all say in the beginning and then they leave."

"How many ways do I have to say it? I'm not going anywhere."

"They say that, too!" Her breath caught on a sob. "They say it over and over. They go and then they come back with more promises until finally they don't bother to make promises at all any more because *they don't come back.*"

"That's what happened to your mom."

"And Lucy." She swiped at a tear. "Her husband didn't even bother to show up for his baby's birth. Remember? So please tell me, why should I believe any of *your* promises?" She knew she was getting ugly, her face was hot from crying, but she didn't care. It was all coming out and she had no way to stop it. The lid was off. The brew of her emotions churned and frothed, boiling over the sides, spitting as it hit the fire below.

He put a hand up like he was going to touch her, then dropped it back to his side. "I love you. And even if I didn't, I don't walk away from my responsibilities."

"And what happens... what happens if you die?"

"*Querida*— "

She shook like a drug addict denied her fix. "Are you going to promise me you won't die like my father? And what happens when I go crazy? What happens when I can't take care of myself?"

The questions came fast and furious, pouring over

the sides quicker than she could push them back in. "What happens when I can't protect the baby? What happens when the baby is killed because I couldn't stay awake? What then, Lucas? What then? Who's going to be there when I fail? Who's going to be there when the police come? Who's going to lie to them? Who's going to keep the secret? Who's going to protect them? Who? Who?"

Lucas caught her as she stumbled, then crumpled, sinking to the floor with her. He rocked her as she cried, her small fist pounding into his chest. Holy fuck. What the hell had happened to her? He soothed her as best as he could, mumbling nonsense words and cradling her against him. He'd never seen her like this and it scared the shit out of him.

"I can't have a baby," she mumbled against his chest. "I can't protect it. I can't."

"Shh, *querida*. I'm here. I'm right here."

She hiccupped on a sob. "I can't do it. I know you'll hate me, but I just can't do it."

He drew her back and smoothed the hair away from her face. "You're stronger than you think. I know you don't believe me now, but I'm here for you. If you're pregnant we *will* work this out together. We will."

She shook her head.

"You don't have to believe me now," he repeated, wiping her tear with the pad of his thumb. God. Seeing her like this nearly broke him in two. He put his forehead to hers, hoping she'd see how serious he was. "One day you will. I won't let you down. I'll do more than promise you, I'll show you."

"I don't want to be like my mother." The pain in her voice reached down inside him and clawed, raking him raw and bloody.

"You're not like your mother."

"What if I am? What if I have a baby and become just like her? I can't do that, Lucas. Even if it doesn't happen with the first child, it could with the second or the third. I can't do that to my children. I won't have my children sleeping in the hall!"

"What the hell are you talking about?"

She pushed at him. "Never mind."

"No, not never mind. Tell me."

"I'm sorry."

"I'll accept your apology on one condition. Tell me what happened to Ethan."

She started to pull away, untangling herself from him both physically and emotionally.

"Who killed him?" he pressed, standing as she did.

Her eyes wide, she put her palms up for him to stop. "I don't know what you're talking about."

"You asked me what happens when the baby is killed. Were you talking about Ethan? Did your mother kill Ethan? Is that what you're afraid of, killing your own child?"

She shook her head, edging away toward the bathroom. "I don't want to talk about this any more. I need to get dressed." She dashed into the bathroom, closing and locking the door behind her.

He didn't make an effort to stop her. Fucking hell. He ran both hands through his hair. No wonder she understood his feelings about his grandfather, she had the same about her mother. They had the same fucking nightmare in common. So much was starting to make sense, but there were still pieces missing. He wasn't going to let her out of this hotel room until she gave them up. He slipped on a pair of boxer shorts and sat down at the table to wait her out.

As for the broken condom... he would make good on his promise to be there for Mi and their child. They'd raise it together. Past that, he couldn't think. He had enough to focus on at the moment with the woman hiding in the bathroom. It was stupid, but he knew if he let himself hope, he'd hope for a baby with Mi.

He'd killed a man and possibly made himself a father all before noon. What a brilliant fucking day this was shaping up to be. And now he had to figure out how to get his girlfriend to tell him her deepest, darkest secret or they would never have a chance. Baby or no.

He ordered five different breakfast dishes from room service, then sat back against the head board, alternating his attention between the magazine he was trying to read and the closed bathroom door. The shower turned off right about the time breakfast arrived. He sat for another fifteen minutes or so before Mi finally came out of the bathroom. She stood in the doorway looking like she'd rather be anywhere but where he was. Her hair was wet, combed back from her face, and she'd wrapped a thick robe around herself. The color was back in her cheeks whether it was from the shower or lingering embarrassment, he wasn't sure.

"Are you hungry?" He motioned to the food spread out on the small dining table. "I ordered breakfast."

She gave him a glance that didn't reach his face. "Yes. Very."

He shoved off the bed on the opposite side from where she stood and began lifting the covers off the plates of food. "Take your pick."

She moved toward him. Her robe covered her feet, making it appear as though she floated. She kept the table between them, sitting down in the chair furthest away from him. He gave her the space she wanted, biding his time before he resumed their conversation.

"Pancakes? Eggs Benedict? Corned beef hash and eggs? French toast? Cereal? There's some fruit and sausage as well." He handed her an empty plate, then sat back and watched her debate the choices.

When she'd taken what she wanted, he did the same. They ate in silence, the only noise the clink of silverware and the drone of traffic outside.

"More coffee?" he offered.

"Yes, please."

Weren't they just the perfect dysfunctional couple? He finished his food, then sat back and watched her take a second helping. She kept her focus on her plate, taking her time with each bite. She was stalling. He let her.

"Would you like more pancakes?" he asked.

She looked at the stack with a mixture of longing and revulsion. She shook her head slowly, reluctantly. Her time for procrastinating was over.

"Now tell me about Ethan," he said.

She played with the corner of the napkin in her lap. "I overreacted earlier. I know you'd be there should anything…" She made a helpless gesture with one hand. "Well, you know."

"If you're pregnant."

"Yes."

"Good. I was beginning to think you didn't know me at all."

"I'm sorry." Her gaze traveled as far as his Adam's apple, then away. "It's just that a baby wasn't something I ever wanted."

"I understand."

"Do you?" She looked at him then, her eyes watery and full of self-recrimination.

"*Querida*, I've met your mother. And you met *my* family. We couldn't scrape together one descent parental role model between the two of us."

She sat back in her chair hard enough to jar it. "So you agree that we shouldn't have a baby." Something like disappointment flashed across her face for a moment before it settled back into grim lines.

"No."

"But you just said—"

"I said we didn't have parents good enough to emulate ourselves after, but that doesn't mean we wouldn't make good parents."

"How can you say that?"

"Were you lying when you said I wasn't like my grandfather?"

"No, but— "

"Good, because I believed you. I can't promise I'll be a great father, but I'll try. I think that's all anyone can do. Don't you?"

"That's you."

"*Querida*, I've seen you with Davy and Gooch. Hell, I've even seen you be loving and patient with Tracey and your mother and brother. I can tell how much you tried to take care of them and Ethan. And how crushed you get when you think you're failing the people you love."

He leaned forward, bracing his elbows on his knees. "You care about the people around you. You don't run from difficult situations. You were there for Lucy when she needed you the most. But most importantly, you care so much about being a good parent that you want to deny yourself the opportunity to be one on the off chance you couldn't live up to your own expectations."

He got up, walked around the table and pushed her chair back. Crouching down in front of her, he took her hands in his. "There's no one I'd rather be the mother of my child than you."

She choked back a sob, catching it in the hand she pulled from his. "Don't."

"You were so young when Ethan died. Only fifteen. You did the best you could for him, for your mother. But now it's time to let me help you. You need my help, Mi. Your mother needs more than you're able to provide. Your brother needs to know what happened."

"No, I can't."

"Tell me what happened."

"You don't... you couldn't understand."

"I didn't think you would understand about *Abuelo*," he answered simply. "But you did."

"It's not the same thing!"

"No. It's not. What were you talking about when you said you wouldn't have your children sleeping in the hall?"

"I never said that."

"Yes, you did. What did you mean?"

HE WASN'T GOING to let up, Mi realized. He would keep asking questions, keep after her to tell him what happened. Well, if that's what he wanted. That's what he'd get. And then he'd see how stupid it would be for them to have a child together. He'd leave her alone. He'd stop making her think she could have the things normal people had. He'd go and have a relationship and a baby with someone who wasn't tied down to the past like she was.

Only she hated the thought of Lucas with someone else, of him holding a child some other woman would give him. Oh, God. Her chest hitched, the tears backing up behind her eyes faster than they could fall.

"I slept in the hall every night," she said, her words coming out as broken as she felt. "Ethan was so small. He... he couldn't help crying. He was just a baby. So small. She... one night he cried. I went to him like always. Can't wake Mommy. But she... she was already there, standing over the crib. She had a pillow. She had it over Ethan. I stopped her. After that I slept in the hall.

Someone had to protect him. He was so small, just a baby. I can't..."

He cupped her face in his hands. "You're doing fine. I'm right here. You slept in the hall to protect him..."

"Yes. Only I was so tired. Night after night in the hall. That night... *that* night I failed. I fell asleep. I didn't mean to. I was just so tired." She clamped her eyes closed tight, the memories of that night streaming by like buildings past a moving train. Ethan. Her mother. Jason. Flicker, flicker, flicker.

"I don't know why I woke up," she continued, pressing her fingers against her eyelids, against the images. "Maybe it was the quiet. Quiet when there should have been noise." She rocked back and forth just the way she used to rock Ethan when he couldn't sleep. "My mom's door was open. I always closed it so she wouldn't hear him cry. I went into his room..."

She bolted off the chair, away from Lucas. She couldn't be near him when she told this part. The room was suddenly too small. He was too close. It was all pressing in on her, crowding her chest.

"I need air. It's too hot in here." She clawed at the robe, yanking it open.

He went to the windows without a word and opened them.

When he made a move toward her she shook him off, backing into the corner. "Stay there, okay? Just stay over there. I need air. It's too hot." She fanned herself with the open robe. Had she ever been this hot?

"Take easy breaths, *querida*. You're hyperventilating. That's it. Good. Take your time."

"It's so hot." She wiped the cuff of the robe across her forehead.

"Do you want some water?"

"No. Give me a minute." She bent at the waist, gripping her knees. This was the hard part. This was the part she'd never told. Oh, God. Her breakfast threatened a reappearance. She moved to the bed and sat down, putting her head between her knees. She would not throw up in front of him again. After a few moments, her stomach offered an uneasy truce, settling enough so she could sit up.

Lucas was there across the room, looking like he'd dash to her side if she needed him. How had she ever doubted him? He'd been there for her in ways no one else ever had been. He was tall and strong, honorable and honest. Despite everything, he loved her. And she loved him right back.

She held out her hand to him. "Come here."

He came to her, taking her hand and easing down on the bed beside her.

She placed his hand between both of hers and began again, focusing on their joined hands. "I went into Ethan's room. My mom was sitting in the chair rocking him. Only... Something wasn't right. I don't know how I knew. I just did." She plucked at the hair on the back of Lucas's hand. "She said... she said that the demon came and took Ethan. She held him up saying that she'd told me that would happen. It was my fault the demon took Ethan. She pushed him at me. His body hung from her hands all wrong. His head bent back like it wasn't supposed to. His face b-blue.

"She said… she said the demon came and took her baby. She pointed at the crib and said, 'He left *that* behind as punishment.' I was crying then, begging her to let me have Ethan. I thought if she gave him to me I could fix him. But she wouldn't. 'Go look,' she said. 'Go see what happens when bad girls don't listen to their mothers.' It was my fault, she said. She said that over and over. '*Your fault*. It's *your fault* the demon came. *Your fault* he left the bad omen behind. Go look,' she yelled. 'Go see what you did.'"

Mi pitched into Lucas's chest and was immediately wrapped into a hug. He murmured sweet things to her, sweet things she didn't deserve. It was her fault Ethan was dead. All her fault.

She had to finish it, get it all out. "I went to the crib. She wouldn't give me Ethan until I did. There was a stuffed bear sitting in one corner. And then it hit me what she was saying. The bear was the omen. The demon left the bear and took Ethan. The demon… the demon was my brother. Jason killed Ethan."

CHAPTER 10

Thirteen years she'd kept the secret, not ever realizing how much of her she'd given over to it, how much of her had been eaten away by it. Expunging the secret left behind a vast empty space she didn't know how to fill. It was as though a chunk of her life had been ripped from her, leaving a yawning gap that should be filled with memories of a life well lived. Would she always carry this emptiness? Would she always be less?

"How can you be sure it was Jason who killed Ethan and not your mother?" Lucas asked.

"Jason never went into Ethan's room," Mi said. "He was only ten at the time, but he resented Ethan, never wanted anything to do with him. There was no reason why his bear would be in there."

"Are you sure? I'd be more apt to believe your mother did him harm than ten-year-old Jason."

"I wasn't sure then and I'm not sure now. I don't know who killed Ethan."

"Did you ever ask Jason about the bear?"

"No."

"Why not?"

She moved to the window, looking out at the traffic on the street in front of the hotel. "Jason had a lot of problems. Even before Ethan was born. He did poorly in school and was bullied. His father drifted in and out of Jason's life until he went to prison for armed robbery. Before he went away Jason lived with him for a short time. I think during that time he might have been molested. Maybe even more than that, I don't know. All I know is that when Jason came back to live with mom and me, he was different, angry and withdrawn."

She turned back to look at Lucas, leaning against the window. The air felt warm and wonderful across her skin, so out of context with the memories she relived.

"He ditched school, stole, lied, and started walking in his sleep. And then Ethan came along, stretching what little money we had even thinner. Jason had to quit his baseball team. He loved playing baseball. I got him odd jobs doing yard work or whatever to help pay the bills. Mom was... well, a lot like she is now. At ten, Jason was pretty much left to fend for himself."

For that, Mi would always feel guilty. Between her mother and Ethan, she had no more room to take care of a ten year-old boy. She'd let him down just as surely as his parents had. Maybe even more so since she was all he had left.

"I caught Jason in Ethan's room once," she said softly as the memory came stealing back, bringing with it more blame, more shame.

"And?"

"I was doing some housework before bed. Ethan started crying, then stopped before I could get to him. Jason met me in the hall, holding Ethan. He was sleep-walking." She paused, this next part was hard to tell. "I asked him what he was doing. He said... he said the baby had been bad and he was throwing him away. I don't know if he would have done it or not, if my running into him in the hall had prevented Jason from doing that or something more. I just don't know."

MI LOOKED AT LUCAS BLEAKLY, all the color leached from her face. Lucas ached to reach out to her, but every time he started to rise she'd turn away from him, shutting him out. Maybe she just needed space to unload years and years worth of heartache and pain. The fear her fifteen-year-old self must have felt was unimaginable. The degeneration of her youth could be pinpointed to the birth of her youngest brother, yet when she talked of him it was only sadness he heard. Sadness and regret.

He'd seen the progression of it in the photos from her house, the stealing of her life, her family and security. Secrets had replaced the usual teenage trappings of dances and friends, homework and dreams of the future.

"The next morning Jason didn't remember any of it. Nothing," she continued. "I tried to keep watch over Ethan, but my mom got by me that night. Jason could have, too. I just don't know."

"So you didn't say anything when the police came."

He was beginning to understand her mindset, why she'd kept these secrets locked away for so long.

"No. I never talked about it with anyone until right now. I know you think I'm wrong for what I did, not reporting my suspicions. What choice did I have? Tell them my mom killed Ethan? They'd throw both Jason and me in foster care while my mom went to jail. Jason was all I had left. I had to protect him. The last time he left us he got hurt."

"Is that why you didn't tell them your suspicions about Jason?"

"Jason had no memory of what he did when he walked in his sleep. How could I tell the police my suspicions? He was only ten. They would have taken him to jail. What if I was wrong and it was really my mother? What would have become of him then? Who should I have chosen, my mom or Jason? What should I have done? If it was my mom, Jason and I would go to foster care and maybe never see each other again. If it was Jason, he would've gone to jail."

"But they ruled Ethan's death as Sudden Infant Death Syndrome."

"How do you know that?"

"Malcolm."

She folded her arms across her chest. "I should have known you'd have me investigated. Well, if you know so much then tell me the rest."

"That's all I know."

"Right."

"What did you do?"

"What did I do? The only thing I could. I put Ethan's

cold little body back in his crib. I gave my mom a sleeping pill, and put Jason's bear back in his bed with him. I laid down next to my mom on the pull out couch in the living room. I didn't cry. I didn't pray. I just stared at the ceiling, wondering which one of my family members killed Ethan. In the morning I picked up the phone and called the police. I gave them a story they believed. And then I did what I could to keep what was left of my family together the only way I knew how."

She seemed to run out of steam, dropping into the chair by the window, her arms and legs loose, looking at nothing in particular.

"What about now?"

"Now?"

"The police believed Ethan's death was by natural causes. Why keep the secret?"

"Why? Because there's no statute of limitations on murder. The threat of foster care is gone, but not jail. If I was sure my mother killed him then yes, I might take the chance of what she'd say or do in therapy. I just can't do that with Jason's life."

"So you'd rather he be angry with you and your mother than know the truth?"

"I'd rather not give him more to deal with than what was forced on him as a child. What good would it do to tell him I think he killed his brother? How would that help him?"

"Letting him shirk his responsibilities to you and your mom is helping him? Letting him keep the resentment he's built against you and your mom helps him deal with what happened when he was a kid? He's a man. He needs to start acting like one. You're preventing him from doing that."

She sat up in her chair. "Don't you think I know that?"

"Do you?"

"You think I like how he treats me? You think I like how he lives his life? You've seen his apartment, he doesn't even care enough about himself to keep it clean. He barely holds down a job. If he's ever had a girlfriend I've never met her. I don't even know if he has any friends. He moved out when he was nineteen and has hardly spoken to me since. I know it's not because he doesn't need anything. He doesn't want anything to do with mom or me. He'd rather starve than spend time with us or owe us for anything."

Her voice caught on the last sentence and he could see how much her brother's estrangement hurt and angered her. He had to press his point here, even knowing how much she'd balk. The thought of her living one more day with what she's had to deal with was more than he could stand.

"You need to tell him. He has a right to know. None of you have moved on from that night and none of you will unless you tell them everything."

"Haven't you been listening? I can't."

"You have to."

"And what if he hates me more for telling him?"

"That's what you're really afraid of, isn't it? That he'll hate you instead of just pitying and resenting you."

"Shut up," she said, her whole body crying defeat.

"You know I'm right."

"You don't know anything!"

"I know that you and your brother will never have a chance at a real relationship until you face your past, work through it, and eventually get past it. Your secret has put a wedge between you and your brother and now it's putting one between you and me. You need to decide what you want more: your secret or your relationships. Until you figure that out no one will be able to get close to you."

"They pass out psychology degrees with discharge papers in the Navy?"

"Think about it. I'm taking a shower." He knew it was a risk, leaving her right then. He expected her to run. She wasn't tied to him anymore, now that Gann was dead. With every step he took away from her, the feeling she'd leave him grew and grew until he closed the door behind him and it sunk into certainty.

What was that stupid saying? The one about loving someone enough to let them go and if they come back they're yours, but if not they never were?

That guy was a fucking idiot.

Mi put the cat carrier down on the floor inside her entry-way. She'd taken his cat. How pathetic was she? She'd stood there in the hotel room, staring at the closed door of the bathroom, wanting to rip it off the hinges and pound her fists into his chest. Instead she threw her stuff into the bag, grabbed his cat and split. Real mature. Of all the ways she'd pictured their break up, catnapping had never figured in.

His furniture was still here, all fragile glass and sharp-ened steel. The house should have been musty from being closed up for so long, but it had a fresh, clean smell. That too was his doing. She wanted to be mad at him for it, add it to the pile of all the other things she was angry with him for, but she couldn't muster the energy.

She was just so tired, having barely enough energy to set up a makeshift cat box with some newspaper and the lid from a cardboard box she'd used to keep back taxes and receipts. Once that was done, she set out some food and water, then let the cat out of the carrier.

"Well, Gooch, this is it... your new home."

The cat sniffed his way out, crouching down low. She picked him up and showed him the cat box and food, then locked the front door. Her bedroom was basically the same, all of her furniture was there, but most of her closet and drawers had been emptied and unpacked at Lucas's. She stripped down to her underwear and climbed into bed. Although it was only noon, the emotional void of unleashing her secret had weakened her, leaving her bone-deep tired.

Staring at the familiar ceiling, she tried for sleep. The mid-day light coming through the blinds zebra-striped up the wall and ceiling, a mocking reminder of how out of kilter her life had become. She rolled over first one way then the other. Her bed—so comfortable before—now seemed lumpy and lonely. She felt itchy as though her skin didn't quite fit any more. Everything was wrong.

Her conversation with Lucas played in a loop through her mind, highlighting over and over how right and yet how wrong he'd been. She couldn't tell Jason. Yes, he was a man now, but when she looked at him all she saw was that ten-year-old boy who still slept with a bear and was so falsely overconfident and wild-eyed with fear that he held himself apart. He'd never brought a friend over to play or asked to go the park or the movies, none of the ordinary things boys did at that age. He did his work, then went to his room.

She never knew what he did in there, respecting his privacy and space. Maybe she should have knocked on the door, checked on him. Every time she thought to do it, her mother or Ethan would need something and all thought of the quiet boy behind the closed door was replaced by infant care and catastrophe avoidance. It wasn't fair. None of it. Not to Mi or to Jason or especially to Ethan, who never lived to see a single birthday.

It wasn't fair, but it was their life. It was all they had except for each other and in the end even that hadn't been enough. The last semblance of family unity they'd shared was at Ethan's funeral when they'd stood—the three survivors—next to a too small coffin at the side of an open grave. Their mother cried big, copious tears, her sobbing echoing the cry of a crow perched on a nearby headstone. Jason had slipped his hand into Mi's, staring dry-eyed into the hole where their brother would soon go. She didn't know if his gesture was for her or for him, but it was the closest they'd ever gotten to any real show of affection between the two of them.

She had many regrets where Jason was concerned and Lucas had stirred them all up with his questions and opinions. If Lucas had thought telling her secret would free her, how wrong he was. The secret was out, but she was far from free. Letting it go had left an empty space, allowing anything that wanted inside to come in and take up residence. The sides of the hole were slowly caving in a grain at a time, back filling the gap with regret, resentment and rage. So much rage.

For Lucas, for Jason, for her mother, and for herself most of all. She'd wasted so many wishes for a different life that she'd long ago given up the practice. But as she drifted closer to sleep, she sent out one last wish.

THE SHARP TRILL of her cell phone jolted Mi awake, startling her out of a dreamless sleep that was as black as the night outside her bedroom window. Her heart tripped again when she read the caller ID. Jason.

"Hello?"

"Where are you? I'm bringing her over. I can't handle her when she's like this."

She climbed out of bed and switched on the light to look for some clothes. "What's she doing?"

"She keeps trying to leave. The last time my neighbor brought her back after she pounded on her door. It's three-o'fucking-clock in the morning. I don't need this shit."

"I'm back at my house."

"I'll see you in ten." He hung up.

She sifted through her closet and came up with an old pair of sweat pants and a promotional t-shirt from a condom company that read, *Smile, it's the second best thing you can do with your lips.*

Jason must have run every red light because he knocked on her door five minutes later. As soon as Mi opened the door, Jason was through it, towing their mother by the wrist.

His gaze flicked to the bruises on her neck, then away as though they shamed him. "I've had it. I'm done with her and so are you."

"Jason, don't speak to your sister like that." Faye glared at him, hands on hips. "I didn't raise you to be disrespectful to women."

"*Now* you're lucid?" Jason shot back. "I've been up and down three times tonight, chasing after you, and you choose *now* to round up all your marbles?"

"Don't talk to her like that," Mi scolded. "Mom, why don't you go lie down in the spare bedroom while Jason and I talk?"

Mi waited until their mother was out of earshot before she turned back to her brother. He was examining Lucas's furniture as though it had come over on the space shuttle. "What the fuck is going on here?" he said with the first real smile she'd seen on his face in a long time.

"That's Lucas's furniture from his apartment. We, ah, kinda switched temporarily."

"Switched?"

"It's a long story."

"I bet. You know, I actually kinda like that guy."

Of all the things he could have said, that was probably the last thing Mi expected. "You do?"

"Yeah." He turned back toward her. "He's good to you and he agrees with me. What's not to like?"

She shook her head. "Come into the kitchen. We can talk in there."

Jason flipped a kitchen chair backwards and sat down, propping his arms across the back. Mi started a pot of coffee—she had a feeling it was going to be a long night.

"You look like hell," Jason said, pitching his voice low.

"Thanks."

"I mean it, Mi. You look like shit. Even without those bruises on your neck, you don't look good. It's not that asshole, is it?"

"No, and stop calling him that. I thought you liked him."

"I do. And as long as he continues to be good to you, we won't have a problem." He fidgeted in his chair a little, giving away his discomfort. This was new.

Crossing her arms over her chest, she leaned back against the counter and regarded him with open astonishment. "Who are you and what have you done with my brother?"

"Shut up."

"No, I mean it. Not that I'm complaining. I like this side of you, but what's going on? Are you trying to butter me up to take Mom back? Because you don't have to. She can stay here with me now that I'm back home."

"It's not like that."

"Then what gives?"

He picked at some chipped paint on the back of the chair with his thumbnail. "That guy really seems to care about you. You deserve someone like that, someone to take care of you. That's all. Don't make any big deal out of it."

She couldn't help the wry smile that tugged at the corner of her mouth. "I'm glad you like him, but we sort of broke up. So I'll be back to taking care of myself again. And Mom."

"No shit?" He actually looked disappointed. "It was because of Mom, wasn't it?"

"No. Look, can we not talk about Lucas?"

"Don't tell me *you* broke up with *him*."

"Jason." Her exacerbation and exhaustion drew his name out as a warning.

He put a hand up. "Got it. I'll just say this and then I'll drop it. Go get him back. Don't let this shit with Mom break you guys up."

"It's not. It isn't." But it was and she knew he could read it from her expression. "Thanks for dropping Mom off. You can go home now."

"I'm spending the rest of the night here. In the morning we're taking Mom to a hospital. I'm done with this, Mi, and so are you."

"Jason." Panic pitched her voice higher than she it meant to.

"I'm doing it and this time you're not going to stop me. She could have killed you. That's all I've thought about since you dropped her off. What if I leave her here alone with you and she goes for you again? There's no one here to stop her. I couldn't live with myself if something happened to you, Mi."

"You can't do that."

"Why not? What the fuck is going on with you that

you can't see how sick she is? Even your Neanderthal of a boyfriend can see it. Hell, half my neighbors can see it. Why can't you?"

"I do see it!"

"Then what the fuck, Mi?"

She'd gotten so used to seeing that look on his face, she hardly noticed it any more—disgust, mixed with pity and impatience.

"I'm doing it and you're not stopping me," he said with a new forcefulness and sense of purpose.

"Jas, please."

"That's not going to work on me anymore. I'm doing this." He stood up and shoved the chair back under the table.

"Don't." She went to him, gripping the front of his shirt with both hands. "I can't protect you if you do this."

"What are you talking about, protect me? Protect me from what? You're the one who needs protecting. *She tried to fucking kill you.*"

"You don't understand."

He pried her hands from his shirt, taking them in both of his. "Then make me."

CHAPTER 11

This was it. The moment Mi feared most and wanted least. She stood toe to toe with her brother who was almost a foot taller and just as stubborn as she was. Something new and ironic set his features in stern lines and flowed through his voice like an angry river—a sense of responsibility.

"I don't need protecting, Mi. You do."

She shook free from his hands. "I'm fine. I've been alone, dealing with Mom for years."

"Maybe so and that's on me. But I'm here now to fix that."

"What's going on with you? Why the sudden change?"

"Let's just say that I got schooled by an outsider on how I'm not living up to my responsibilities to my family."

Lucas. Had to be. He must have said something to Jason at his apartment while Mi was out of the room. "What did Lucas say to you?"

"Stop treating me like a kid. What do you think you'd be protecting me from? What could Mom say or do that could hurt me?"

He wasn't going to let it drop. Perhaps he had changed. He certainly seemed different, standing up to her, as he'd never done before. Whatever change had occurred in him either because of what their mother did or what Lucas said was definitely for the better. He wasn't going to back down. Pride swelled within her, making her smile.

"What are you grinning at me like that for?" he asked.

"I really like this side of you, that's all."

"Whatever."

He pulled the chair out again and dropped down into it, stretching his long legs out in front of him. She had the strongest urge to ruffle his hair as she used to when he was a boy. But he wasn't a boy anymore. Lucas was right. Jason was a man now and needed to be treated that way. She'd failed him when he was a child; she wouldn't fail him now. She grabbed some mugs and poured two cups of coffee. She sat them on the table and retrieved the cream, setting it next to the sugar bowl and cups of coffee.

Jason watched her, sitting up straighter in his chair as she sat down at the table with him.

"I need to tell you some things, but before I do I want you to know that I did the best by you as I could, the best I knew how. I know I made a lot of mistakes and I'm sorry. I hope you can forgive me one day." She focused on her clenched hands on the table.

He placed his hand over hers. "I know that, Mi," he said gently. "You're the only one I had to depend on. You saved me a thousand times. I know I've been a jerk to you. I'm sorry." He slid his hands back and picked up his coffee, but didn't drink. He stared into the dark liquid as though it was a crystal ball. "We both got screwed, but you especially, having to take care of an annoying kid, a baby, and a crazy mom. I couldn't do anything to help back then, but I can help now. So whatever you have to tell me, I can take it."

She could see that he could or at least he wanted to. She hoped he'd feel the same after she turned his life upside down. "It has to do with the night Ethan died."

He didn't seem surprised or make any other indication about how he felt as she told him everything, leaving nothing out. When she got to the part about his sleep-walking with Ethan in his arms, he just nodded along, absorbing her words as truth. The old Jason might have thrown up excuses or railed back, wanting to shift the attention away from himself. This quiet, contemplative Jason threw her at first until she realized how much she'd needed him to be just like this.

By the time she finished, he just stared straight at her, his jaw flexing. His coffee had grown cold, but he still held onto the mug with both hands.

"Now you know why I did what I did with Mom," she said. "And why we can't take her to a hospital tomorrow or ever."

"That's still happening."

"Jason, no."

"I said no more, Mi, and I meant it. This doesn't change anything. Maybe she'll say something, maybe she won't. Either way, it's over. I can't let you sacrifice your life anymore. You're not my shield. I'll take what I've got coming."

He pushed the mug away, rising to his feet. "I can never repay what you've done for me. For Mom and Ethan, too. But I can start by taking care of Mom. Go get your life back, Mi. Go think of yourself first for once. And for fuck's sake, go make up with that asshole, Lucas, if he's who you want. I can take care of myself. Thank you, but I don't need you to protect me any more."

She stood up, too. "You don't know what you're saying."

"Yeah, I do." He took her by the shoulders with hands that shook. "This is over, Mi. Let me do this. I need to do this for you. I need to do this for Mom and for me." He cleared his throat, fighting back the emotion and tears shining in his eyes. "Mi, please." He echoed the words she'd always used on him to get him to do what she wanted.

"I don't know whether I should hug you or kick your ass," she said without any real heat.

"Come here." He wrapped her in a hug. His body felt foreign to her and she realized she couldn't remember the last time they'd really hugged.

They parted and he pulled a folded up piece of paper out of his pocket. "I did some research on hospitals. I circled a couple of places we could try. Have a look and let me know what you think."

She was so dumbfounded, she couldn't speak just stare up at him as though she'd never seen him before. And maybe she hadn't. He'd finally grown into a man she could rely on to do the right thing.

"Good night." He dropped a kiss on her forehead.

She watched him walk down the hall and poke his head in to check on their mom before heading to the bathroom at the end of the hall. She fell heavily into the chair and unfolded the paper. He'd printed it off a computer, a list of hospitals in and around Dallas. She still couldn't believe the change in her brother.

She fingered the bruises and scratches on her neck. A blessing in disguise? Maybe. But she couldn't help being afraid for them all. What would happen to their mother? Would she talk about the night Ethan died? Would she finally get the help she needed and become the mother she and Jason should have had?

Smoothing the paper out on the tabletop, she realized the wish she'd sent out before falling asleep might really have a chance of coming true.

LUCAS HUNG up the phone with a sense of purpose he hadn't felt since leaving the Navy. He and Malcolm were starting their own business, an offshoot of Malcolm's private investigation firm that would branch out into security consulting and protection services. He'd just gotten off the phone with a former SEAL buddy of his who had agreed to work for their new company. It was all coming together.

He'd spent the past few weeks working on this new venture. After a long, difficult conversation he had finally gotten *Abuelita* to agree to let Carmen continue running the company. She knew it best and had taken it in a new direction that would be very profitable for them all. Now he was free to pursue his own business, something he hadn't known he'd wanted to do.

The security breach at his apartment building that had allowed Doyle Gann to get to Mi had haunted Lucas. He'd taken that failure personally, had dogged Detective Rolls until he'd figured out exactly what had happened. Gann had used Lucas's neighbor's key card to get into the building and with a few tweaks, into Lucas's apartment. Lucas had taken the information Rolls had given him and had studied the security system, which led to the discovery of the flaws that had allowed Gann access.

Saving the document of proposal he'd been working on for his first potential client, Lucas closed his laptop. His training and knowledge was being put to good use with this new venture. He now had everything. A new career, a new sense of purpose, and a new business. Yeah, he had everything. Everything except the one thing he wanted most—Mi.

She hadn't called, hadn't stopped by to pick up any of her stuff. He'd heard from Cal that the show had begun taping again in a new studio. The sick fuck that he was, he'd actually tuned in to the show every night at two in the morning just to see her. He could have DVR'd it, but no, he had to see it as it aired as though it was a live broadcast and hadn't been taped earlier in the day. She looked good.

Who was he kidding? She looked amazing, beautiful. He found himself staring at her image, remembering how they'd been together. How they'd ended things. He wondered if she was pregnant and if she was, would she tell him? He rubbed his thigh, wishing he had DVR'd at least one of her shows so he could watch it right now.

Fuck.

He slid the file Malcolm had dropped off to him a few days ago toward himself. He hadn't given Mi much of anything, but he could give her this. Inside were copies of the police and coroner's reports on Ethan's death. There was no new information in the coroner's report. The police report was another matter. Mi deserved to know what was in it. He should call her, invite her over, and show it to her.

He picked up his phone as he'd done a dozen or more times since she'd left the hotel, intending to do just that, then changed his mind and set it back down. He went to the kitchen instead and grabbed himself a beer to sit down in front of the TV to watch the Ranger game. He clicked the TV on and flipped through the channels. The beer was cold and just right after the long day he'd had.

"Got another one of those for me?" a familiar voice asked.

He jumped up and spun around nearly dropping his beer. Mi stood just inside the entryway to the living room with the cat carrier in her hand. She looked even better than she had on her show. He drank her in, noting the bruising around her neck had faded. Her hair hung long and loose around her shoulders. Her eyes, Jesus fuck, her eyes glowed amber, reflecting the golden light of sunset coming in through the windows.

He swallowed hard, willing his mouth to form words. "You stole my cat." That was not what he'd intended his first words to her to be after all this time. Idiot.

She offered up the carrier. "I brought him back."

He stood rooted to the floor like a giant awkward oaf, staring at her as though she was a mirage. "I see."

She glanced at the couch, then at him. "You kept my furniture."

"Yeah. I guess I did."

She took a couple of steps closer so that they were separated by nothing more than the depth of the sofa. She leaned over and sat the carrier down on the cushions. When she straightened she seemed nervous, biting her lower lip. "I just thought you should know that I'm not pregnant."

"Okay." He couldn't keep his disappointment from showing either on his face or in words. He'd more than hoped, he'd dreamed. He knew she saw it by the way her gaze slid toward the television.

"Well, that's all I really had to say. I guess I'll go now." She nodded toward the TV. "Enjoy your game."

"Wait!" He came around to her side of the couch. "I'll get you that beer."

"All right."

He made it to the kitchen and back in record time. He handed her the beer, feeling like a nervous teenager on his first date. "Have a seat."

They rounded the couch from opposite sides. He put the cat carrier on the floor and opened the door. Gooch hissed at him, then bounded off, probably to piss on his bathroom rug like he used to do. Sitting a foot away from her after all this time did something funny to Lucas's stomach. He set his beer down on the coffee table and turned to her.

"Cal tells me you're back filming the show. How's it going?"

She smoothed her thumb over the label on the bottle, giving it all of her attention. "It's different. I really miss Davy, and Tracey, too, although I know I shouldn't. Crosby isn't the same; he's quieter if you can believe it. I guess none of us will be the same." She gave a helpless shrug. "I guess that's normal."

"How are your mom and Jason?"

"They're good. Mom won't ever be normal, but she's doing okay. She'll likely need to be in a psychiatric facility the rest of her life." She looked at him then and he got that punch in the stomach when their gazes connected. "We found a hospital that would take her full time. It was Jason's idea. He's changed. I guess I have you to thank for that."

"Me? How's that?"

"He said, and I quote, 'I got schooled by an outsider on how I'm not living up to my responsibilities to my family.' I'm guessing that outsider is you. So thanks."

"You told him about the night Ethan died?"

"Yeah. I hadn't intended to, but he came to my house with Mom and said he was putting his foot down. He was taking control of the situation. He said that when Mom choked me something changed in him. He realized he needed to grow up and take care of his family. I'm really proud of him. That night he brought over a list of hospitals he'd looked into. He really took the initiative."

"How did Jason take the story of the night Ethan died?"

"He didn't back down. He said it didn't change

anything. He wasn't going to take any more chances of me getting hurt and that no matter what happened to him, he wanted me to have my life back. He even told me to, and again I'll quote him, 'Go make up with that asshole, Lucas, if he's who you want.'"

"Yeah? I guess that kid's not half bad after all."

"No, he's not. He's really coming into his own. He visits Mom a lot and talks to her doctors. He won't let me do anything other than visit with her. I feel guilty for being relieved about that."

"Don't. You've paid your dues and now you need to let him take over the responsibility for a while."

She laughed. "That's what he says."

"So are you?"

She paused, the bottle part way to her lips. "Am I what?"

"Making up with this asshole."

She opened her mouth to speak, then shut it again, resting the bottle back in her lap. "I'm sorry. I shouldn't have left the hotel room without saying goodbye."

Oh, shit. He'd read her visit all wrong. "I understand."

"I owe you so much. I want to thank you for what you said to Jason that spurred his turn around. And for convincing me to tell him everything. My life has changed in so many ways. It's taken me a while to get a handle on things, but now I go out with friends a couple of times a week. I started seeing a counselor, which was something my mom's doctor suggested. I feel really good. I'm getting happy and I have you to thank for that." She raised her bottle in toast. "So thanks."

"You're welcome, although I can't take all the credit."

"You have to take some."

He remembered the file on his desk. He supposed it would be his parting gift to her now instead of the entry back into her life that he'd hoped for. "Wait here. I have something for you."

Walking the short distance down the hall to his office, he tried not to think, concentrating on putting one foot in front of the other until he was sitting back down next to her. "Here." He handed her the file.

"What's this?"

"The information Malcolm gathered on Ethan's death."

"Oh." She looked as though she didn't want to take it.

"There are copies of all the reports. It doesn't look like foul play was ever suspected although there is a note on the police report I think you should read." He flipped through the pages until he came to the one he wanted to show her. "Right here."

"My father had a sister? Oh my God. I never knew that. My mom never told me."

"I did a little more digging. I hope you don't mind." He pulled a piece of paper from the back of the file. "Her address, email, and phone number. She lives in Oregon with her husband. They have three kids and two grand-children. She's expecting your call."

"I don't know what to say." And she didn't need to. The look on her face was worth the effort and more. "Oh, Lucas. Thank you. Thank you so much. I owe you more than I could ever repay."

"No. You don't. I was glad to do it." Here it was, the goodbye she hadn't given him in that downtown hotel room. He could feel in coming, like the low rumble of a Humvee in the distance. He rubbed at his thigh.

"The answer's yes by the way."

"The answer to what?"

"To making up with this asshole. If you'll let me."

He could hardly think for the pounding of his heart. He wanted to pounce on her, smother her with kisses, but she was still talking.

"—to come here free of all my problems. That's all I had when we started before. I mean, let's face it. I was a mess. I'm less of a mess now and you already know all my secrets. I still have a few things to figure out, but I'm here and I want to try again." She paused. "If you want to."

"We'll try again as what? Fuck buddies?" Idiot! What was he saying? He'd take her as anything she wanted, any *way* she wanted.

Pressing her lips together, she set her beer down on the table next to his. "If that's all you want then... no."

"Good, because I want so much more from you than that, *querida*."

She let out her breath, her words coming out in a whoosh. "Oh, thank God. I was so afraid I'd lost you. I love you, Lucas." She threw herself at him, wrapping her arms around his neck. She kissed him, tasting of beer and that indefinable something that was all her.

He pulled back to look into her amazing eyes, falling for her all over again, drawn into her invisible force field. "*Te amo, querida. Te amo siempre.*" I love you. I'll always love you.

*

Thank you for reading SAVED! The next book in the LOVE STORIES series is FAKE .

Cal and Lucy fake a marriage, but their feelings for each other are very *real*. A second chance, enemies to lovers romance.

➤CLICK HERE TO READ FAKE

If you enjoyed SAVED, please consider leaving a review on your favorite book site. Reviews help readers find books!

➤SAVED, A DANGEROUS LINES NOVEL

➤GOODREADS

Join my VIP Facebook group Babes with Books for exclusive sneak peeks at my upcoming books & other, members only, perks:

➤www.facebook.com/groups/BabesWithBooksReaderGroup

Sign up to receive my newsletter for new release alerts, exclusive bonus content, and giveaways!

➤**www.bethyarnall.com/newsletter**

Turn the page to read an excerpt from FAKE now!

EXCERPT FROM FAKE

Lucy Monroe stood outside the thick wooden door with the gleaming brass nameplate, preparing to beg someone she couldn't stand for something she didn't want. Tugging at her slightly too-tight blouse, she hoped she hadn't overdone the perfume in an attempt to mask the stale stench of desperation. And desperate she was or else she wouldn't be standing outside of Cal Seller's office door.

Tossing back her hair, she rubbed her lips together and took a deep breath. She raised her hand to knock, pulling the gesture at the last moment before she rapped on the chest of the man who suddenly opened it.

"Well, hello, Lucy." Cal set his hand on the door-frame, blocking her entrance with six feet of lanky, over-confident cowboy. If he was surprised to see her, he didn't show it. His gaze traveled over her leisurely, not stopping to admire anything in particular as though he'd seen the view a thousand times before. Her body reacted as if he'd stroked her, aroused despite her burning hatred for him.

When he'd looked his fill, he stepped back, motioning her into the room. "Come on in."

"Er, ah, thank you." Chin high, she strolled into the room like she had a right to be there and hadn't told him to shove the job she was here to get back where the sun don't shine. As though she hadn't rubbed her new marriage and pregnancy in his face with the giddy glee of a teenager who'd snagged the star quarterback and wanted her cheating ex-boyfriend to know it. *Oh, how the mighty have fallen*, she thought. And fallen hard.

"Have a seat." Cal waited for her to be seated before sliding into the high-backed, leather chair at his desk. Behind him the Dallas skyline gleamed in the heat of mid-day. He reclined back, regarding her with those same cool blue eyes that used to rake her over as if he could see through her clothes. "What can I do for you?"

He'd asked her that same question before under entirely different circumstances. Naked and panting circumstances. Teasing and pleasing circumstances. Right here on top of his desk, her legs hooked over his shoulders... She cleared her throat and those memories from her brain, struggling to keep in mind the real reason she'd come here today. Her daughter, Poppy.

"You're going to need a new host for *Pleasure at Home*. At least temporarily. I can help." There. That didn't sound desperate, it sounded helpful. She was doing him a favor really. And if that favor turned into a permanent job for her, then so much the better. Cal loved win-win situations. Especially if he was the one doing all the winning.

"You're looking for a job?"

She was looking for more than that. What she needed

was a miracle, a way to hold on to what little she had left. "My daughter will be eight months old next week."

He inclined his head in acknowledgment. Of course he knew that, nothing passed Cal's notice.

"I thought it was a good time to venture out and explore my options." Which were exactly zero. Unless she counted working retail with its long hours and measly pay. And how would she protect Poppy if she was never home?

"So you ventured my direction."

"I figured with Mi going out on maternity leave in a few months I could fill in for her. It's not like I'd need to be trained. I cohosted the show with Mi for two years before...before I left."

"Yes. I remember."

This wasn't going well. She could tell by the way the right corner of his lips had tugged up along with his eyebrow as soon as she'd opened her mouth about resuming her old job. She used to call it his *oh really* look. That mocking, *I'm in the driver's seat* tilt of his lips and brow set off all the warning bells inside her. He was plotting something. Something dangerous for her.

She stupidly plowed ahead anyway, too needy to walk away from what might be her last chance. Her only chance. "Yes, well, I thought I could start right away. Mi and I could cohost like we used to until she leaves, and then I could host alone until she comes back." And hopefully she could parlay that temporary into permanent.

"What happened to your... How did you put it? Ah, yes. Your husband's aversion to his wife prostituting herself by selling sex toys on TV."

"That was an unfortunate choice of words on my part. I apologize."

"Unfortunate. Yes. But still a problem for you, unless something's changed?"

The bastard. He knew. And now he was tormenting her by trying to make her confess what an idiot she'd been, how her life had crashed and burned. She thought about her daughter, and all her prideful anger drained away, leaving her more desperate than before. She'd do anything to protect Poppy. Anything.

She picked at the skin beside her thumbnail, knowing she had to tell him in order to get him to give her back her old job. An extremely well-paying job. A job she needed more than her next breath. "I'm not married."

"I thought you didn't believe in divorce."

"I'm not divorced."

"An annulment?"

"No." Damn him. "It turned out my marriage wasn't legal."

"Not legal? It seemed perfectly legal from where I sat in the church."

She'd invited him out of spite. She imagined he had attended out of pride. Their relationship—so passionate and exciting—had ended in barbs and jabs meant to wound. Now that too was coming back to bite her in the ass. *Keep your cool. Don't let him see you sweat. He thrives on the weaknesses of others. Don't be weak.*

"I thought so too," she said, sounding more confident than she felt. "Unfortunately he was already married when he married me."

"I see."

"So there's no conflict. I can start right away, or whenever you need me."

"But I don't."

"Don't what?"

"Need you."

She bolted up out of her chair, toppling it backward. "You son of a bitch! You let me sit here and spill my guts to you, knowing all the time that you weren't going to hire me back?"

"Sit down."

The door behind her opened. A willowy brunette with the body Lucy used to have poked her head in the door. "Is everything all right in here, sir?" She cast Lucy a look like she'd be happy to have her escorted out.

"Everything's fine, honey," Cal answered.

Thank God this wasn't *the* Honey Cal had employed back when Lucy had worked for him, but she was made from the same mold. Cal called all of his assistants *Honey*, and they all looked like they'd been ordered from the *Playmate of the Month* catalog. Rumor was that Cal's *Honeys* did more than run reports...a lot more. Unfortunately Lucy knew all too well the rumors were based in fact.

Cal's *Honey* gave him a look that could melt ice in a snowstorm. "You let me know if you need anything, sir. Anything at all."

"Thank you. I will." Cal waited for *Honey*—or Felicia McAdams as the nameplate on her desk read—to close the door before turning his attention back to Lucy. "Please, sit down."

She folded her arms across her chest. "Why? So you can humiliate me some more?"

"You need a job, and as it happens I might have one for you."

"But you just said you didn't."

"I said I don't need you to fill in for Mi. Her sister-in-law will start cohosting with her today and then take over while she's on leave."

"So what's the job then?"

"Sit down and I'll tell you."

Cal waited with the patience he used to close multi-million-dollar deals for Lucy to right her chair and sit her pretty little ass back down. Truth was he knew why she was here and what she was going to ask before he'd even opened the door to find her standing on the other side. His gut twisted, thinking how desperate she must be knocking at his door. It was his fault she was in the straits she was in. He'd kept tabs on her, but apparently not close enough.

She'd shown up sooner than he'd expected, but as it turned out she'd come at a time when he'd just gotten his ass handed to him and was feeling a bit beaten up. Funny that sparring with Lucy had him rebounding with the energy of a champ. She always brought out the best in him. And the worst.

Lucy sat at the edge of the chair and crossed her arms and legs. "Well?" she demanded.

Now this was going to take some finesse. He'd been chewing over this predicament for some time and then he'd opened the door to Lucy and the solution had very nearly tumbled right into his chest.

"It's a bit high profile," he began.

She squared her shoulders and lifted her chin. "I've been on TV. That's the tiniest bit high profile."

Damn, but he'd missed her spirit. And her smart-assed mouth, and the way she tossed her blonde hair when she expected to get her way. He'd missed a whole lot of things about her, including the way his body reacted to her.

"The hours are fairly flexible," he continued. "You have a reliable babysitter who can work days and evenings?"

"I do."

"Good. Good. And you don't mind dressing up?"

She narrowed her eyes at him. "What kind of *dressing up* are we talking about?"

Now she had him remembering the time she'd worn that pretty little cowgirl outfit and had ridden him bare-back...backwards. It fit with what she thought of him, he supposed. Pervert, bastard...what else had she called him? Ah, yes. A lowlife, two-timing son of a bitch with a dick for brains.

Maybe she was right. He certainly hadn't been able to accurately access the head he *should* be using ever since she'd strolled into the room and stroked him with the scent of her perfume.

He leaned back in his chair, stacked his boots on his desk, and clasped his hands in his lap. The blue of her eyes was barely visible now. She'd narrowed them into slits that told him his window for possibly winning her over with his idea was quickly closing.

"Not that kind of dressing up." He'd keep this to business if it killed him. "Cocktail dresses, ball gowns that sort of thing."

She tilted forward in her chair a little and uncrossed her arms to stack them on her knee. He hadn't gotten to where he was now without being able to read an opponent's body language to know when things were starting to swing his direction.

"Would they be provided?" she asked. "Or would I have to come up with the money to rent them out of my salary?"

"They would be provided. You'd have an expense account for whatever you'd need."

"And what exactly would my duties be?" She was interested. Good.

"Charity events, dinner parties, corporate functions, hostessing, that sort of thing."

"Sounds more like something you'd need a wife for than a corporate employee."

"That's exactly what I need. A wife."

*

Want to read more?

➤One-click FAKE now➤

If you loved SAVED, you'll love the sexy, funny, award nominated RECOVERED INNOCENCE series. The first book in the series is VINDICATE.

Cora's brother was convicted of a murder he didn't commit and it's up to her to set him free. Inspired by real cases taken on by The Innocence Project.

★ Nominated in 2017 for the Romance Writers of America Rita® award★

➤One-click VINDICATE now➤

Looking for something lighter and funny? Check out THE MISADVENTURES OF MAGGIE MAE series, starting with WAKE UP, MAGGIE, available now! Maggie has to keep her very inappropriate thoughts to herself about the FBI Special Agent assigned to protect her from a murderer.

➤One-click WAKE UP, MAGGIE Now➤

ACKNOWLEDGMENTS

Writing is a solitary endeavor, but without the help and support of my friends and family I would never have realized my dream.

Alison Diem, Charity Hammond, and Debra Mullins are the greatest critique partners ever. They've been a part of this book from the glimmer of the idea to The End. They've helped me become a better writer, picked me up and dusted me off more than a few times, and managed to convince me that I was not writing drivel when I was absolutely positive I was. Thanks ladies.

When published authors take the time to help an unpublished author it is a true and rare gift. Thank you Vicky Dreiling and Susan Squires for your invaluable help. My undying gratitude to Debra Mullins and Shannon Donnelly, I've learned so much about story telling and writing from both of you. I promise that one day I *will* master the semi-colon.

My thanks to M.A. Taylor, who helped me with my law enforcement questions. Any errors are mine not hers.

A special thank you to my husband and sons for eating lots of frozen pizzas and fast food and for making it possible for me to pursue my dream. I'm working on that swimming pool for you boys.

ALSO BY BETH YARNALL

Dangerous Lines

Lost

Saved

Fake

Real

Urge

Rare

Betray

Recovered Innocence

Vindicate

Atone

Reclaim

The Misadventures of Maggie Mae

Wake Up, Maggie

You're Mine, Maggie

Find Me, Maggie

Azalea March Mysteries

Killing It In Vegas

Beth Writing as Betty Paper

Crazy On You

Captive

Tinsel

Piano Lessons

BETH'S BOOKS FOR WRITERS

Crafting Unputdownable Fiction series

Going Deep Into Deep Point of View

Making Description Work Hard For You

Some Like It Hot: Writing Sex and Romance

ABOUT THE AUTHOR

USA Today best selling author and Rita® finalist, Beth Yarnall, writes mysteries, romantic suspense, and the occasional hilarious tweet. She lives in Southern California with her husband, two sons, and their rescue dogs where she is hard at work on her next novel. For more information about Beth and her novels please visit her website- www.bethyarnall.com

facebook.com/bethyarnallauthor

amazon.com/author/bethyarnall

bookbub.com/authors/beth-yarnall